LIKE CLOCKWORK

A YOUNG ADULT TIME TRAVEL ROMANCE

LEE STRAUSS

la plume
PRESS

LIKE CLOCKWORK

by Lee Strauss

(previously published under the names Elle Strauss and Elle Lee Strauss)

THE CLOCKWISE COLLECTION

Dedicated to the fans of
Clockwise and ClockwiseR.
You rock!

ONE

ADELINE SAVOY

MY DAD STILL THOUGHT I WAS TEN. That was how old I was when my mother died, and how old I was when my father crawled into his "cave," also known as his office on the 26th floor of the John Hancock tower. Six years later, like a bear coming out of hibernation, Dad decided his days of hiding behind a desk were over. I thought he was going through a mid-life crisis, which was why we now lived in Hollywood instead of Cambridge. And why when I spotted his reflection in a mirror at the cosmetic counter in the Shop & Save store, I almost dropped the *Scarlet Passion* lipstick tester I'd just smeared on my lips.

Even though I was sixteen, I wasn't allowed to wear make-up. True. With my left hand I used a tissue to wipe the evidence off my mouth, all the while watching my dad's familiar profile move in and out of range in the mirror.

He was laughing. I crouched down and turned, my vision just missing the counter top, and watched. His hair had grown out since the "decision." He used to always keep it so short, that I didn't even know it was wavy before, and the lines on his face never used to turn upward in a smile.

I had to see who was causing this cosmic reaction in my father. The clerk who sold cheap jewelry, a pretty-in-a-fake way brunette, tilted her head and giggled back.

My jaw dropped and something really strange started happening in my stomach. I felt a little sick because I couldn't believe what I was witnessing. My dad was *flirting*!

Who was this man dressed in khakis, flip-flops and an untucked pseudo Hawaiian shirt? My real dad only wore pinstriped suits with starchy white shirts and a blue tie. Always. Even to bed, I was certain.

"Miss? Are you all right?" The cosmetic clerk was armed with a spray nozzle cleaner in one hand and a paper towel in the other.

I mimed as best I could, "ssh", but apparently dad was the only one with acting skills in my family, since she wouldn't leave me alone.

"Miss? You don't look too good. Should I call for medical?"

The fake pretty lady stopped chatting when she heard her colleague talking so loudly. Obviously, that meant my dad's little flirtation episode was over. And of course, my blonde ponytail was a giveaway. "Adeline?" he said.

"Dad!" I jumped up, feigning surprise.

"What are you doing here?" he asked.

What are you doing here? I thought. "Um nothing, just looking. Thought I might buy some gum."

Dad glanced back at the fake and I did a quick switcheroo, replacing the tester and grabbing a sealed golden tube. It tucked nicely in my fist as I crossed my arms over my chest.

"Adeline, come here," Dad said. "I want you to meet someone."

My legs moved toward dad and the fake without my permission.

"Adeline, this is my friend from acting class, Spring. Spring, this is my daughter, Adeline."

Spring extended her hand. Unfortunately, the contraband lipstick was in my right hand. I wasn't a magician. Dad would notice if I tried to switch. I opted for the awkward offering of my left hand.

"It's so nice to meet you," Spring gushed.

"Same," I said, not meaning it at all. "Not that I don't want to stay and chat," I added quickly, before Dad could draw us into more forced intimacies, "but I've got to go."

"I'll walk with you," Dad said. But he wasn't looking at me; he was smiling at the fake.

"It's okay, Dad. I'll meet you at home." I strutted across the floor to the cashier. He glanced back at me as I stood in line at the register. I waved the pack of gum in the air. I paid for it and the lipstick while Dad and the fake went back to making googly eyes.

I SNAPPED the gum in my mouth while caressing the lipstick tube in my hand. It was encased in a plastic protective seal, a perforated strip running the length of it like a zipper. My thumb picked at the rim. All I had to do was rip it open and it would no longer be returnable.

But I really should return it. I'd promised myself I'd give up the greasy lip habit when we moved. It was a chance to start over, do everything new, and be a proper daughter with a proper father.

Hrumph. Like that was turning out. Dad wasn't exactly holding up his end of the bargain.

My breaths came out short and rapid, like a panting dog. I didn't realize how fast I'd been walking. I'd hardly taken in the tall palm trees that lined the road or the sweet smell of tropical flowers I didn't know the names of.

No signs of autumn in sight. In Cambridge the leaves would be showing signs of turning color, bright reds and yellows. A little twist in my stomach. I was homesick.

And angry.

He was supposed to change, but not like that. He was supposed to notice me, spend time with me, not some flake called Spring. What kind of name was that anyway? It sounded like a made up actress name. Her last name was probably Storm or Wind. My thumb picked the plastic a bit more.

"Hi, there."

I turned my head. Some guy riding a pink bike with a sparkly white banana seat and matching tassels that hung off tall, wide handlebars slowed down to keep pace with me.

"Hi," he said again. This time there was no mistaking he was talking to me.

"Hi?" I said, not slowing down at all to do so. I may be entering my junior year, but I still didn't talk to strangers. Janice, my babysitter/pseudo mom in Cambridge, had drilled that lesson into me good.

"My name's Marco. I live next door to you."

Okay. I slowed a little. "Why are you riding a girl's bike?" Did he steal it? Why didn't he care about how stupid it made him look?

"It's my sister's. I sold mine to buy something else, but riding this is better than walking."

"I'm walking and you're not making any better time than me." I was annoyed. Why didn't he just keep going? I preferred to sulk alone.

"You're new, so I thought with school starting tomorrow, you'd like someone to ride the bus with."

Good point. Who knew what kinds of Hollywood weirdos would be on the bus? I looked Marco up and down. He was average height, shaggy hair, and wore a graphic T-shirt and surfer shorts with fat, loosely tied skate shoes on his feet. No socks. He had nice, tanned skin and warm brown eyes that squinted to almost close when he smiled. He wasn't hard to look at.

And he looked trustworthy enough, I guessed. Plus, he was right. I didn't really want to go to Hollywood High alone.

I stopped and turned to him. "I'm Adeline Savoy." I wiped the sweat on my right hand off on my skirt—sky blue, slightly flared and to my knees—and offered it wanting to start my new friendship off on the right foot.

"Cool," Marco said as we shook. "You like to make things official. I like that."

The sun must've glinted off the gold tube in my other hand because Marco nodded toward it. "What'ya got there?"

"Oh, it's just lipstick. I bought it, but now I'm not sure. I might take it back."

"I don't know why girls wear that vile stuff," he said. I was surprised by the strength of his statement.

"It makes us feel good. Pretty. What's wrong with that?"

"For one thing, you're already pretty without it."

He thought I was pretty?

"Besides," he continued, "it's made out of horse urine."

"It is not! That's so gross."

"It is. That's why it has that sticky consistency. Have you ever seen dried urine around a toilet?"

"You're disgusting! How would you know about lipstick, anyway?"

"I have three sisters, though one is only six years old and hasn't discovered the evils of make-up and this culture's drive to sexualize young girls. It's too late for my older sisters, but you can still be saved."

Who was this guy? And how did he get off talking to me like that? He didn't even know me.

I felt my lips settle into a tight line and my pace picked up.

"Hey, I'm sorry. I didn't mean to offend you."

How long was he going to walk with me? "Where did you say you lived?"

"Right next door to you."

"Right next door?" This annoying person, who happened to be my only friend, lived right next door?

"Yeah, the two-storey. My bedroom window faces yours."

"You see in my window!"

"No. I don't..." His face flushed red.

"You do, you *do* look in. You peeping Tom!"

"Adeline, I didn't see anything. I just heard your music."

"Huh?" I stopped and spun to face him.

A grin tugged at the corners of his mouth. "And your singing."

"What?" I was mortified. He probably heard me singing along to *Feist*, or even worse, he saw me doing my Michael Jackson impersonation. I bet he saw me doing the *Thriller* dance the other night. Ugh!

"Everyone can hear you. You have your window open."

"You know what? Don't talk to me."

Marco seemed truly taken aback, and yet he didn't get the hint. Not even one as direct as that. He was not only a peeper, but he was dense, too.

"I live in a house full of women. Three sisters and a mother. I get what's going on here. It's PMS, isn't it?"

Was he *kidding* me? As if I would talk about something like that with him! I stopped and stared hard into his eyes. I produced my new tube of lipstick and slowly peeled the perforated strip, letting the plastic wrapper drop to the ground. I dramatically popped off the lid and twisted the base until the bright red dried horse urine was in full view.

Then I put it on my lips, slowly, purposefully, first the top and then the bottom, smacking them in Marco's direction when I was done.

Take that, Mr. I Know Women.

Marco bent down, picked up the plastic wrapper and pushed it in his pocket. He straddled the bike and pushed off, turning back long enough to say, "I'll pick you up at 8:10 tomorrow morning for school."

Argh.

TWO

I FUMED THE REST of the way home. First, about my dad and the flirt, and then about Marco the peeping Tom/annoying neighbor. Pebbles of aggravation rubbed against my rib cage forcing my mouth to drop open in a low growl.

Deep breaths, Adeline. I knew what strong emotions could do to me. I counted to ten. I entered the gated community we now lived in—one and two-storey Mex-Tex homes with salmon colored stucco and red tile roofs. Each one had a small front yard patio dotted by citrus fruit trees and desert cacti. The lemon tree in ours was a selling feature for someone like me who was born and raised in the northeast.

I had to dodge a wayward ball belonging to some kids playing road hockey in the cul-de-sac. One of them yelled, "Car!" as the neighbor across the street pulled out of his driveway and honked the horn.

Before I squeezed on the wrought iron handle that opened our front door, I paused to stare at the two-storey home to my right. Dark cotton curtains with a spaceship print fluttered through an open window on the second floor. Marco's room. Figures he still had a child-themed décor. And yes, now that I took the time to look, he did have full view of my room from there.

I'd have to keep my blinds closed from now on and shut my window when I played music, just in case I broke into song without thinking, which obviously, I was known to do.

Someone to my left cleared her throat. An elderly woman sat out on the front patio of the one-storey on the east side of our house. I didn't notice her behind the tall bushes in her yard. She wore a fine print dress with a white, soft-knit sweater draped over her shoulders. Her gray hair was covered with a straw hat, and she had light pink lipstick on her lined lips.

For that reason I liked her.

"Hello," I said.

She smiled crookedly, but said nothing. Maybe she didn't speak English, though she didn't look Latino. Then, I noticed how the left side of her face sagged, and how her left arm lay limp on her lap, and thought sadly that this sweet woman had suffered a stroke. I wiggled my fingers at her before unlocking my front door and going in.

Everything in our new house was bright and colorful, with tiles on the floors, counters and bathroom walls—so different from our colonial home in Massachusetts.

Cardboard boxes still cluttered each room. It had become my job to unpack and redecorate, since Dad was immediately busy with his acting classes. I had to give the guy credit. He knew how to go after what he wanted.

I just wished it were me.

Where was he anyway? Wasn't he supposed to leave the

Shop & Stop right after I did? I'd expected him to overtake me with those long legs of his.

Erg. It was the fake. Really, I couldn't see what he saw in her anyway. She was nothing like Mom was.

I sat on a chair in front of the mirror and examined my face. I looked like my mother had at my age if her photographs were anything to go by. An oval face with wide set blue eyes and a full mouth to match. Except the image staring back at me lacked the softness of my mom's expression. At least the expression I remembered. It was foggy to me now, what Mom looked like before she died, and it scared me. Most of my memories were somehow tied to photographs. I grabbed the five by six I had of her and me at the beach. She had her arms wrapped around me from behind as we sat on a bleached log, our matching blonde hair tangling up together in the wind. Yes, this was what she looked like, but I was losing my memories. A familiar lump formed in my throat.

I heard the front door open and slam shut again.

"Adeline?"

"In my room," I called. I didn't want my dad to come searching for me.

"Come help me decide on dinner," he called back.

My dad didn't cook so I knew it would be a choice between two kinds of frozen.

"Coming."

I plucked a tissue from the box on my dresser and brought it to my mouth to wipe off the lipstick I'd put on to annoy Marcos, then paused. I still had the golden tube of *Scarlett Passion* in my hand. If Dad could re-invent himself here in Hollywood, then why couldn't I?

I put the tissue down, opened the tube and applied a nice thick layer of red to my lips.

MY DAD HELD up two trays with food images on them. "Chicken Linguine or Thai Noodle?"

"I don't care. You pick."

He took a deep breath in, like this was a life altering choice. "Let's do Thai. I'm in the mood for spicy."

He looked at me after turning the oven on.

I waited. It didn't take long.

"Are you wearing—lipstick?"

"Yeah, so? I'm sixteen now."

"Sixteen's not eighteen. You look like a tramp."

"Dad, you're exaggerating."

"No, I'm not. Go take it off."

I left but I didn't go to my room. I settled in on the sofa and clicked the remote. *Frazier* re-runs.

"Hey, Dad. Your favorite show."

Instead of sitting next to me and analyzing every line and nuance like he usually did, he put on that stern parental voice.

"Adeline, I asked you to do something."

"I heard you, Dad. And I think it's too late for you to start inputting in my life. I've been wearing lipstick for over a year now. It's no big deal."

What had gotten into me? It wasn't like me to challenge my dad. My only goal since Mom had died was to please my father in any way I could.

Had I really stopped caring?

Dad stood between me and the TV. "Adeline, now!"

I crossed my arms and shook my head. We were having a

showdown. My beating heart jumped into high gear, in part from fear—I didn't know my father well enough to know what he would do—and in part from anger. It was a feeling I knew all too well—this bubbling fury from deep in my gut. I'd become a master at suppressing it. But, lately the monster had been creeping out, slithering, like goo and impossible to contain.

"Dad."

"One, two..."

He was counting? *Counting*? "I'm not three years old! What are you going to do, spank me?"

That stopped him. He pointed his finger and opened his mouth but nothing came out. I could tell he was at a loss, and I predicted my victory.

But, I'd have to wait to find out for sure. I grew dizzy and my body seized with a sensation of falling as I was thrust into a tunnel of white light.

I'd wondered when it would finally happen. I was surprised, actually, that it took two weeks. I just wished I could've finished (and won) the fight with my dad first.

I stood in an empty field; thistles and sage brush scratched my bare legs. It was a wide-open space, but at least I could see the edge of civilization. I started walking. Let's see what "Old Hollywood" was really like.

Starting over was both frightening and exciting. Back in Cambridge I knew the cards I'd been dealt. Maybe it wasn't the greatest hand, but I knew how to play it. Here, I'd have to learn a brand new game.

Would I find friends here? People who would help me along even though I'd keep disappearing from their lives at regular intervals? My chest tightened at the thought of being alone. If I didn't fit in here, I didn't fit in anywhere. I certainly didn't fit in at home with Dad.

By the time I reached the outskirts of town, my legs were marked with fine red lines from the scratchy weeds. I took a moment to rub the itch and discomfort from them.

I crisscrossed through the intersections keeping a north westerly direction and before I knew it I was on Sunset Boulevard. It was still busy and colorful, but old. Yet new. Weird. The streets were wider with fewer lanes, and the buildings were newer and glitzier and with more space in between, like they could breathe. Modern Hollywood was run down, graffiti ridden and congested in comparison, like a drunken movie star fallen from grace.

No one really paid me any attention. I had the dress code down, which was why I wore a lot of skirts and flat shoes. In my time anything went, and in Hollywood, as far as I could tell, the weirder the better. It was helpful that I could wear whatever I wanted and retro was a good look by most people. So, my clothes didn't shout out "foreigner," or worse "alien," as in space cadet.

My hair was pulled back in a ponytail at the nape of my neck. I reached back, loosened it and re-tighten it higher up, like the girls I'd spotted across the street at the Orange Julius stand.

I smiled at all the "old cars" running up and down the streets and parked at the curbs. I'd seen them before, of course, in Cambridge, but in Hollywood, everything seemed to have an added flare. I kept my eyes peeled for movie star sightings, and could swear I saw William Holden enter the bank.

I passed by a hair salon and stared at the pictures in the window. Short was definitely in. Short with a ring of curls, like a hat rim, and a cowlick thing happening with the bangs. I twisted my long hair around my finger. Should I go shorter?

Before I knew it, I was inside.

Things definitely went around and came around. Like the color lime green. The door, walls and even the back splash tiles behind the sinks were green. Each black, patent leather chair had a big beehive-looking hair dryer poised over it, all pink. The windows were covered with light lacy sheers intended not to block sight, but sunlight.

I liked it. It was feminine and welcoming.

"Hi, ya," the lady with scissors said. "I'll be right with ya." She was tall and slender, and had short dark hair just like the models in the photos in the window. She wore a short-sleeved, finely knitted top that covered pointy breasts (the brassiere style of the times) and a long fitted pencil skirt that ended mid-shin. She attacked a pile of hair with a broom.

"They come in spurts, y'know? Everyone wants their hair cut at once, and then nobody. I tell them to make appointments, but for some reason, they don't think I'll be busy? Why, I ask? They don't think I'm good enough to stay busy? Then how come I'm always busy?"

I just shrugged and wondered if maybe I misjudged the place. Should I take off while I still could? After all, I hadn't made an appointment.

The woman patted the back of a chair. "Well, come on, honey, sit down. I'm ready."

"Uh, actually," I nibbled on my lip. "I haven't decided yet."

"Ah, yeah." She nodded her head knowingly. "All the kids go through this. They want to go shorter because they think they'll look older, but they're still attached to the long hair they've had all their lives. It's okay. I'm not busy, *at the moment.* Come sit down, look at the magazines, and if ya change your mind, y'can leave. No questions, no charge."

Where else did I have to go? "Okay." I took the three steps necessary to get to the nearest salon chair and sat down.

"I'm Faye," the woman said, handing me a hair magazine. Up close I could more accurately gage her age. I'd guess somewhere around her late twenties, early thirties.

"I'm Adeline."

"Well, welcome, Adeline. I don't think I've seen y'around before and I've lived here my whole life, so I know most of the folk." Faye paused to check her face in the mirror. She pulled a lipstick tube out of her front pocket and applied bright orange. I smiled.

"I'm new," I said.

"Really? Who's your family? Maybe I've met your mother."

"My mother passed away when I was ten." Might as well throw the sympathy card on the table right off.

"Oh, I'm so sorry." She pouted sympathetically. "You sweet thing and already without your mother. My mother passed away two years ago, and I miss her terribly." Faye settled into the salon chair next to me. "How's your father coping?"

After today's flirting episode at the Shop & Save, I wasn't sure. "Um, okay. It's been a while now."

"Do y'live near here? Maybe I should meet him? I could bring over a casserole or something?"

Was she just being kind? Or was she scouting? My dad was too old for her, not that she'd ever actually meet him. "No, we're way across town. In fact, my father travels a lot for work."

"Oh," Faye said, "is he a *Fuller Brush* salesman?"

I shot her a blank look.

"You know, the men who sell brooms and mops door to door?"

Sure, why not? I nodded my head. "Yeah."

Faye reached over and touched my arm. "You can stay for supper with me. I hate eating alone. I mean, sometimes my brother drops by and sponges off me, but I never know when that'll happen."

The bell over the door rang. A red haired woman (short hair, of course) came in.

"Faye, darling, do you have time for a trim? My hair is driving me mad."

Faye slid out of her chair and offered it. "Anytime, Betty."

Seeing me, Betty said, "I don't want to jump in line."

"I'm not a customer," I said. "Not yet. I can't decide."

"Betty, this is Adeline. She's new. She doesn't have a mother and her father's one of those traveling broom salesmen."

"Oh." Betty didn't look like she knew what to do with this info. "Well, nice to meet ya."

Faye and Betty caught up on the daily town gossip while I took a stroll around the salon. I hadn't noticed that the shop was actually attached to a little house. An open door near the back revealed a small clean kitchen.

"Kids nowadays," I overheard Betty saying, "they listen to that God awful Rock n' Roll music. I just cover my little ones' ears when they drive by with their radios blasting."

"I don't know," Faye countered. "I kind of like some of it. Puts me in a good mood, makes me feel like dancing."

I peeked through a window that looked out at a side yard. An old truck drove in, rattling and puttering, and came to a stop. The driver's door opened and my jaw almost fell off my face. Out popped the most beautiful man I'd ever seen. He wore jeans rolled up near the ankles and a tight white T-shirt accentuating a well-built body. His hair was slicked back off his face, which was a fine, chiseled specimen. He was definitely channeling his inner James Dean. This was 1955, maybe he was James Dean. When did JD die, again? I'd have to look that up as soon as I got home.

Faye said her brother sometimes dropped in for supper.

"Faye," I called over my shoulder. "Who does your brother look like?"

Betty chipped in, "James Dean."

Yes!

"Why," Faye said. "Is he here?"

I nodded, glassy-eyed. Faye caught my look. "Oh, no, Adeline. He's too old for someone like you. Besides, Howard ain't nothing but trouble. Y'best stay away from him."

Hey, I could handle trouble. Look at my life. And if trouble looked like that, bring it on!

Howard opened the hood and started fiddling with the engine. I propped my elbow on the window sill, rested my chin in my hand and just watched the beauty of it all, every flex of his biceps, every wrinkle of his brow.

"Oh good Lord, Betty, there goes another one," Faye said. "Really, I don't get the attraction."

"That's because he's your brother, honey," said Betty. "I can see why the girls all go la-la after him. He's the cat's meow."

Yes, he is.

Howard glanced my way. I jumped back, but it was possible he could still see me because he never turned away.

Then he tilted his head—was he motioning for me to come outside? He raised his eyebrows and nodded.

Yes, he was! He wanted me to join him.

I turned toward the door. Faye stared at me, a scowl forming on her face.

"Adeline," she admonished.

But she didn't have to worry; I wouldn't be hanging out with her brother today. "Faye, I have to go. Thanks for the offer for dinner. Maybe another time."

I stepped outside just in time to disappear.

THREE

WHEN I TRAVELED back in time from the present, it happened in an instant, hardly any warning except for the sudden dizziness and a flash of light. At least I had a bit of lead time when I went to the future from the past. I could feel it coming on, which allowed me a chance to get out of sight before vanishing into thin air. There had been times when I didn't succeed and some poor soul saw me disappear before their eyes, thinking they must be drunk or insane.

When I traveled from the past back to the present, I returned to the exact moment I'd left. No one in my time saw me disappear. No matter how many times I changed clothes in the past, when I returned to the present I had the exact same clothes on I had when I left. I remained in the same place. The only telltale signs were the dark circles around my eyes. And I was usually quite discombobulated.

Like now, sitting on the sofa in my living room, with Dad shouting at me to go to my room. I didn't even remember what we were fighting about. I just got up and went, leaving my dad standing wide-mouth and red-faced.

I shuffled down the white tile floor of the hallway to my room, still not used to the brightness of my bedroom with all the sunshine every day. I closed the blinds and crawled under the pink, satin covers of my white-lace canopy bed—a childhood relic I was unable to let go of because it reminded me of happier times with my mother. I took a short nap before my dad called me back for dinner. Traveling exhausted me.

We ate TV dinners while watching *Mad Men*, *Seinfeld* and *CSI New York*. The latter made me homesick, just with all the east coast flare; dark attire, (none of this pastel cotton wear that overwhelmed west coasters) trees with leaves that fell to the ground and branches that were eventually frosted with snow. Not a palm tree or convertible in sight.

"So, how's it going, Dad? Do you think you have a chance to break in, now that you see how tough it is?" My dad wasn't bad looking, in fact he was better looking now, with his new laid-back persona, than I ever remembered him to be. Maybe because he smiled more. But the fact remained he was *old*.

As if reading my mind, he said, "The competition is worse with all the up and coming twenty-somethings. But the TV watching audience is getting older now, too, mainly because the youth are watching whatever it is that they watch on the Internet." He paused before adding, "So there's more room for older actors." I couldn't tell if he was making a statement of fact, or just trying to convince himself.

"Do you think you can get work, though?" I knew we were living on savings right now, and yeah, my dad had a really high-paying job for a lot of years, but what we were doing now couldn't be sustainable forever.

"I think so. I mean, I'm not expecting to be the next Brad Pitt or Tommy Lee Jones, but I could make it as one of the guys you see in a lot of shows, the ones whose names you never really get to know. I'm not looking to be the next breakout star; I just want to be a working actor."

I couldn't tell if he was shooting too high or too low, but I had to give him credit for trying.

"Why?" Dad said. "Do you think this was a mistake?"

Yesterday, I would have said yes. Today, after meeting Faye and Howard, I thought my travel life was better, if nothing else. Back in Cambridge I'd spent a lot of time with farmers who didn't mind the odd come and go laborer who'd work for cash under the table. Sometimes, I'd pick up old jewelry at pawn shops and flea markets to sell in the past for cash. Old money was hard to come by, and I'd get arrested if I'd try to pass bills printed after 1955. I found a few people in Cambridge who'd help me on occasion, but no one as nice as Faye.

"No, I think we can do well together here." Emphasis on the *together* part.

MARCO SHOWED up at my door the next morning at 8:10 as promised. For my first day of school I dressed in a slim skirt that ended at my shins, flats and a fine knit sweater. I smiled to myself—I looked just like Faye and more like I was heading off to work at an office instead of starting the first day of my junior year at a new school. I was more concerned about being ready to travel back to 1955, if it should happen, than whatever anyone might think of me here.

The old lady shuffled outside onto her patio again and

settled into her chair. Marco called out to her, "Morning, Mrs. Bradshaw."

The lady's eyes twinkled and she waved.

"How long has she lived there?" I asked after we were out of earshot.

"I don't know. She was here when we moved in."

Across the street a frazzled stay-at-home mom was shooing a set of twelve-year-old triplet boys out the door to catch their bus. Marco's mom waved as she drove by. Through the open car window I could see she was dressed nice and her hair was carefully styled.

"What does your mom do?"

"She's a secretary at a big law firm. She wanted to be a lawyer, even made it into law school, but then my oldest sister happened."

It took five minutes to walk to the bus stop.

"By the way," Marco said. "I'm sorry about yesterday. I didn't mean to step on toes."

I barely remembered yesterday. Well, anything that didn't include Howard.

"It's fine. Let's just start over."

"Sounds good. So, do you like sports?"

I looked up at him. He was taller than me and had a better tan than me (I didn't tan—I was a permanent whitey, though I was surprised by the sprinkling of freckles that had shown up recently on my nose. I didn't get those in Cambridge). He wore another white T-shirt, khaki shorts and the same skate shoes as before. A banged up skateboard was tucked under his arm.

I had to admit he was kind of cute, but in a puppy dog sort of way. Not at all like Howard who was pure hot hunkiness.

"Adeline?"

"Oh, I'm sorry, my mind drifted."

"Sorry to bore you."

Our friendship wasn't starting off on the right foot, and since he was the only friend I had, I really needed to put more effort into this.

"I'm sorry, Marco. I have a lot on my mind. What was it you asked?"

"Nothing big, just making conversation."

"So, what was it?"

"Do you do sports?"

"No, I'm not athletic at all. What about you?"

"I like skateboarding." He gestured to the board under his arm. "And surfing. I spend most of my weekends at the beach. I like music, too. I can play guitar."

"Awesome." At first I thought he was going to bring up the whole I-heard-you-singing thing and I felt myself tense up.

"Maybe we could listen to music together sometime?" He said this a little too eagerly. What I didn't want was some kind of crushing going on.

"I don't know, maybe." Thankfully we arrived at the bus stop before he could get weird on me.

It was a popular stop. A trio of girls in short skirts eyed my outfit, disapproval flickering on their faces followed quickly by disinterest. I was a nobody, at the bottom of a very long ladder and no threat to them. Behind a bush, but hardly hidden, were a couple guys with teary eyes smoking up (it wasn't even 8:30 in the morning!), and not far from them, two guys who had to be identical twins, were dressed in Star Wars outfits. They sparred with each other with toy laser swords. They were candidates for making someone like me look cool.

"Are they for real?"

"Yup. Brad and Brett Chazwell, but everyone calls them Bing and Bong. Total sci-fi geeks.

The bus pulled up and everyone got on. Marco took a seat near the front across from a girl with short black spiky hair and piercings in her nose, eyebrow and all the way down each of her earlobes. She was a pixie sized girl, but the "accessory" that stood out the most, the thing I tried the hardest not to stare at was her leg brace.

Marco nodded at her. "Hi, Bluebell."

And I thought I had a strange name.

He took the window seat and patted the spot beside him. I took it. Bing and Bong sat in the seat in front of us. The pretty girls and the stoners went to the back and were joined by jockey looking guys who had to run to catch the bus. The last guy carried a basketball, spinning it on his index finger. By the sound of the giggles coming from the gaggle of girls at the back, someone was impressed.

Even on a bus the pecking order was established. I could see that I had already aligned myself with the nerds.

Which was fine. With my condition, I was better off with fewer friends.

"This is Adeline," Marco said to whoever was listening. "She's new."

"You're into sixties retro?" Bluebell asked.

"Fifties," I said. "I'm really into the fifties."

"Yeah, the fifties were tote cool," Bluebell said.

"Tote?"

"Totally," Marco explained.

We drove east down Sunset, past the main entrance of the school, then left on N. Highland to the school parking lot. Hollywood High was actually a collection of several two-storey buildings, The main entrance off Sunset had a wide cement staircase that led to the front doors flanked with a sign that confirmed the school's name. A grassy sports field was tucked in behind, and the gym had a gigantic drawing of a "sheik" ie: the mascot. The theater that faced N. Highland had the famed colorful banner mural of former students who became stars along the top. It wrapped around the corner turning into a massive two-storey tall mural of John Ritter.

The fence around the theater wasn't your standard chain link, but a metal fence with a row of steel rods, curved like canes—the kind you'd have in a nightmare, with pointy chest probing tips.

Clusters of kids dressed like gang members stood near it, some of them puffing on cigarettes. Boarders hung out on a stairwell inside of the fence, with guys sliding down the rail one after the other until a teacher showed up to scare them off.

At first I thought Hollywood High was really small, a white two-storey building on Sunset Boulevard lined with a row of standard-issue palm trees. When I discovered it was actually a group of buildings that wrapped around onto North Highland and I was filled with a new intimidation. There were quite a lot of expensive cars in the parking lot. I wasn't a car connoisseur, but I could tell when a car was more about the bling than transportation.

Many of the drivers who exited the cars were also exceptionally good looking. Their passengers, too. Everyone had great hair, great clothes and in the case of the girls, great legs. I could tell this because they were basically exposed to just below the butt level, whether shorts or skirts. I felt old fashioned and frumpy in my fifties get-up, and suddenly, I wanted to be invisible.

Marco and Bluebell showed me the office so I could get my schedule and school map. After quick instructions on how to get to my first class, I was on my own. I managed to navigate the crowded halls in the two-storey building with my head down and not kill myself. When I located the classroom, I took an empty seat at the back.

Where I found I got my wish. I was invisible.

Not one person talked to me, not even the teacher when she dropped a worn copy of a textbook on my desk.

Same for Biology and World Civilization. Obviously, there were enough people living in Hollywood now—no need for one more.

By the time lunch came and I found the cafeteria I was super grateful for Marco. He saw me when I walked in and waved me over.

"I got a tray of food for you, since it's your first day, and you probably have enough new things to figure out."

Marco did indeed have two trays with exactly the same food items—Mac and cheese, half a ham sandwich and an apple.

"Thanks, Marco." I pulled a chair out and sat down. Bluebell arrived taking the chair beside Marco (I wondered if she had a thing for him). The way she pulled out the chair and managed her tray of food, with her *less useful* leg (was that politically correct enough?) was excruciatingly slow, and I pictured her lunch splatting on the floor beside her.

Marco didn't offer to help her which didn't seem like him, so I had to figure she didn't want help.

Then, not so surprisingly, Bing and Bong took seats across from us.

"Do people call them Bing and Bong to their faces?" I asked Marco quietly.

"Yeah, they don't mind their nicknames."

Bing and Bong were in a heavy discussion about the Klingon language, testing out their knowledge on each other. None of us wanted to interrupt that.

"What classes did you have, Ad?" Bluebell said.

Ad? No one had shortened my name since my mother died.

"Yeah, Ad," Marco said, his eyes teasing.

Fine, *Marc*. How'd he like it if I changed his name? On the other hand, he didn't suit Marc. He was definitely a Marco.

"Do you like Span?" Bluebell took a bite of her apple.

"Spanish," Marco clarified.

"Yeah, I got that. Uh, it's okay."

"It's an easy credit for me," Marco added. "My mother still chats us kids up in Spanish at home. She doesn't want us to lose it. There's one of my sisters over there."

Marco pointed to a slim girl with long, brown, super-shiny hair and an overly made-up face who was wearing the latest fashion trends.

"Candice thinks she's a supermodel or something. I think she's borderline street walker."

"Marco!" Bluebell said. "That's so har."

Harsh?

"It's true. Candice is just trying to be like my older sister, Lucy. Candice needs to find out who *she* is."

I almost choked on my drink. "Are you a junior shrink or something?" I said.

"It doesn't hurt to understand how people tick, why they do the things they do."

"Yeah, except you sound really judgmental."

"I'm not judgmental. I'm observant."

"I'm with Ad on this one, Marco," Bluebell said. "You can be tote judgmental sometimes."

"I don't judge you, Bluebell. Even though you're mutilating your body, I'm still your friend."

"Using the word 'mutilating' is judgmental," I said. "Maybe Bluebell thinks it's art, or her way of not being like *them*." I pointed to the clan of pretty girls at the best table in the cafeteria.

"You're so true," Bluebell said.

"But, Adeline, *you* just judged all those girls over there," Marco said. "So, if I'm judgmental, so are you."

Marco could be so annoying, but we couldn't get into it any more. The bell rang

"Hey, Ad, wait up!" Bluebell's high pitched voice called after me in the hall. I turned and frowned. I didn't know why it bugged me so much that she shortened my name. The slimy monster in my belly hiccuped.

"I think we're in the next class together," she said, catching up.

"Choir?"

"Yeah. There's only one junior choir class, so when Marco mentioned that was your next class, I knew."

We started down the hall. I thought I'd follow her since I wasn't sure where the class was. With Bluebell's leg, our progress was agonizingly slow. I really didn't want to be late because that would just give the teacher an excuse to *present* me, or *chastise* me. Or worse, make me sing in front of everyone. I only took choir because it was an elective where I didn't have to talk to anyone or write assignments.

Step, drag, step, drag. I hadn't noticed how much effort it took Bluebell to walk before.

"Um, I don't mean to be rude," I said. "But, I really don't want to be late on my first day."

Bluebell looked a little startled, and I could tell I'd hurt her feelings. She feigned a smile. "Sure, no prob. I'll meet you there."

I confirmed the directions and left her hobbling behind me. Part of me knew I had just been a jerk. Another part didn't care. That much.

I was right, though. I got to class in time to work out with Mrs. Foster that I was an alto. She gave me sheet music and asked me to sing. Right there. As people were walking in. I gulped, but did it anyway, but very quietly. I was loud enough for Mrs. Foster.

"Good," Mrs. Foster said, smiling. "Take a spot in the alto section. It's nice to have a strong addition to the choir."

Bluebell made it just as the bell rang. She took her spot in the front row without catching my eye.

FOUR

AFTER CHOIR, I followed Bluebell as she shuffled out. I knew I should apologize, but I'd waited too long. Her next class was across the hall from the choir room, and she disappeared before I had a chance.

Great. Way to alienate my only female friend.

I checked my schedule and school map, looking for my last class— thankfully—of the day. When I looked up, I saw Marco's sister. She was leaning up against an outside wall, talking with a guy. Her face was serious and she made a lot of tense arm gestures. The guy had dark hair and a football build. He wore loose jeans that hung low on his hips. A chain hung between his belt-loop in the front and his back pocket. Though I would call him good-looking, there was something about his eyes that scared me. He smacked the wall above Candice's head. We both jumped.

She slapped his face. He grabbed her wrist, and the way he grimaced, I was afraid I was going to have to break up a fight. Not that I looked at all tough or intimidating, just well, if the guy saw that he had a witness, maybe he wouldn't strike out.

The guy turned and caught me staring. I stared back, and swallowed hard. Chills ran down my spine, but it worked. Candice pulled her wrist free and stormed away. I darted in between the buildings, out of sight, even though it was exactly the opposite direction I needed to go. It took a while for me to swing back and I was almost late for the last class of the day.

Which was gym. Which was destined to be my worst class. The possible physical contact with other kids was hazardous because I could potentially take someone back with me if we touched skin to skin. I learned this the hard way when I was twelve.

When my mom died, Dad kind of handed me over to the neighbors, Janice and Tom Whitemore, a middle-aged couple with two young boys. Janice took me in, in part out of pity and in part because they needed the money, since she stopped working when she had the kids.

Even though she helped me like a mother, we never bonded. She lavished affection onto her boys, Dylan and Dustin, who were three and four years old at the time. I'd never stopped being the visitor, and she seemed relieved every time my dad picked me up at the end of the day.

So, I was twelve and the boys were five and six when Janice bought them a kitten, an orange tabby-cat named Tiger. He was the cutest, fluffiest kitten and so unbiased as to whom he'd show love. He loved *me* as much as he loved them.

Then one day, while I was petting the cat, I *left*. It was the anniversary of my mother's death and neither my dad or Janice, or Tom (he worked a lot and I hardly saw him) even acknowledged it. I had a big hole in my heart all I wanted was my mother back, but instead I just had a cat to pour all my sadness onto. I pressed my face into his and his nose mashed up against my cheek.

Next thing I knew, he was with me in 1951. The bad thing was, when I re-entered, I was sitting on the floor, and no Tiger.

Of course, I couldn't explain what happened or why the cat was nowhere to be found. The boys freaked out. (I never really touched *them* if I could help it. They always had runny noses, and smelt a little off.) I had to help pin up posters with a picture of Tiger on lamp posts all through our neighborhood. Thankfully, about a month later, when I went *back,* I found him. Because I have lead-time on re-entering I had opportunity to grab him first. Tiger safely returned, but a lesson was learned.

So, I didn't like gym because it wasn't a great idea for me to touch people skin to skin on purpose, but also because I sucked at sports. Back in Cambridge I always got picked last for teams.

The teacher put one of the boys in charge of picking teams for a game of soccer. I recognized him from the bus that morning, the last guy on with the basketball. It turned out his name was Paul. He called on me half way through, "The Girl with the Brown Shirt." After today's game I could guarantee I would be the last one called from now on. And probably I would always be known as *The Girl with the Brown Shirt.*

I took my usual position, as far back and as far away from anyone else as possible. I only had to kill forty minutes before it would end and my first day would finally be over.

This was what happened when you didn't pay attention. Suddenly, I was in the middle of all the action. Paul and another boy were fighting over the ball and somehow I got in the middle of it. I tried to get out of the way, but I was like a magnet to them. They pushed up against me, my feet twisted and then I was on the ground with two sweaty guys still fighting for the ball. I kicked back, angrily, desperate to get away from them.

"Get off me!" I shouted. Smelly, heavy oafs. They didn't know what they were messing with when it came to me. I kicked Paul in the butt, hard, and rolled away from the fray.

And just in time. Dizziness and white light.

I was lying alone in the scrub on a wide batch of raw, undeveloped land.

Yes, I was back in 1955! I couldn't wait to see Faye again, and hopefully get another glimpse of Howard. I stood up to get away from the prickles and brushed the dust off my butt. Oh no. I was wearing gym strip. After I had carefully dressed in my skirt and flats today, I ended up here in shorts, an unflattering T-shirt and running shoes.

I had two choices: sit here, wait it out, and risk starvation and/or being eaten by coyotes, or go into town as I was.

I decided to go in.

I looked like a street urchin with my baggy shorts and untucked shirt, and my hair flying away from the soccer field scuffle. Though girls wore shorts in the fifties, they weren't anything like what I was wearing. Shorts in the fifties had high waistbands and side zippers or buttons and were made from stiff cotton fabric. They were paired with feminine blouses, tucked in—the look was still ladylike, not tomboy gone amuck.

I tried to stay out of sight, ducking behind fat, fifties vehicles and tin garbage bins, making my way to the only place I knew—Faye's salon.

The bell over the door gave me away when I tried to slip in. Faye was there, with Betty again, but this time they were sitting in the waiting chairs, drinking coffee and smoking cigarettes.

"Adeline?" Faye said. "Is that you?"

My hand self-consciously went to my hair, trying to smooth it. "Yes, um, I'm sorry, I'll go if you're busy."

"Don't be silly, come in." Faye said this with mild concern still on her face. "Would y'like a coffee?"

"I don't drink coffee, but a glass of water would be nice."

I sat down beside Betty. Faye rested her partially smoked cigarette in an ashtray that looked like a tall, skinny end table with a stand made of twisting brass rods and got me a glass of water.

"Betty was just telling me wonderful news." Faye's face pinched a bit as she said this, like it pained her somehow. "She's having another baby!"

"That's great," I said.

"Number four!" Faye added with animation. She picked up the dying butt of her cigarette and took a long drag.

My eyes went to the cigarette in Betty's hand. "You know," I said, "maybe you don't want to be smoking that with a baby coming."

"Heavens, dear," Betty said, after exhaling a puff of smoke in my face. "Why not?"

I gulped back the water. Getting bowled over during a soccer match made a person thirsty. "Well, I've heard it can be bad for the baby, like they're smoking the cigarette, too."

"Nonsense. That's the silliest thing I ever heard," Betty said, stubbing it out. "Anyway, I must be going. I need to pick the kids up from school and get supper going before Chuck gets home."

"Thanks for stopping by," Faye said. The bell tinkled as Betty slipped out. Then she leaned back to stare at me.

"What on Earth happened to you?"

What could I say that would be remotely believable? Faye wasn't the patient type and didn't wait for me to come up with an excuse.

"It's because y'have no mother, isn't it? Are y'living alone, child? Is your father gone?"

Sounded good to me. I just nodded.

"And y'must be out of clean clothes, I gather. You don't have a washing machine, do ya?"

I shook my head.

"Well, come with me, honey, I'll lend you some of my things." Faye stood abruptly and I followed her to the back door that opened up to her kitchen. On the way by, I glanced out the side window. Howard's truck was still there, the hood propped open. Did that mean he was here?

My face flushed at the thought of seeing him again, and then with mortification when I remembered what I looked like. I pressed out my T-shirt with my hand as if that would make a difference.

"I saved enough money to buy my own Sears and Roebuck washer and dryer; I do my laundry in less than half the time it used to take. I've got a new electric vacuum, and a blender for my kitchen. If it weren't for all these new appliances they're making these days, I wouldn't have time for my salon."

You had to walk through the kitchen to get to the living room. Two doors, side by side on the far wall, stood open. The first to the bathroom and the second to Faye's bedroom. She rummaged through a wardrobe—a closet as a separate piece of furniture and not built into the house—and produced a gray flared skirt and a red cotton blouse with cuffed short sleeves and a rounded collar.

"You can get dressed in here. I'll be in the kitchen."

I changed quickly. I wasn't sure what to do with my dirty gym clothes so I stuffed them under the bed. Then, I took the liberty of borrowing Faye's hairbrush. I brushed my hair until it was smooth and shiny again and tied it back up into a ponytail.

When I presented myself, Faye rushed to me, like she was going to bear hug me, then pulled back as if she thought better of it. Good thing, with a bare armed hug, Faye could be meeting my dad after all. She clasped her hands in front and said, "You look terrific, sweet Adeline. Now come, y'can peel the carrots.

Faye had every electronic appliance imaginable, and was busy frying chicken in a shiny new electric frying pan. All the while she was singing softly.

My Adeline,
At night, dear heart,
For you I pine;
In all my dreams,
Your fair face beams.
You're the flower of my heart,
Sweet Adeline.

She had a really pretty voice.

"What is that you're singing, Faye?"

"Oh, you haven't heard it before? *Sweet Adeline* is a famous Barbershop Quartet song, originally from a Broadway play.

"It's nice," I said.

"It's how I remembered your name from last time. Which

by the way, y'never explained your abrupt departure. Did my brother scare ya off?"

Hardly.

"Um, no, it's just, sometimes, I'm shy. Yes, I can get very, very shy, all of a sudden, and when that happens, I just have to be alone. It's not personal."

"Okay. That's good to know."

"So, speaking of your brother, I saw his truck."

"That piece of junk? I know, and I tell him not to leave it in my yard, but he says he has nowhere else he can park it."

"So, it's not running?"

"Apparently not."

My stomach sunk a little. I'd missed my chance to meet Howard because of my untimely departure. Time travel could be so inconvenient. If only there was a way to control it, a button to push or a knob to turn.

But if that were the case, I surprised myself by thinking, I'd probably never go home.

I set the table for two and enjoyed fried chicken with mashed potatoes and cooked carrots.

"Thanks for letting me stay for dinner," I said. "It's really good." A big improvement from what my dad and I pumped out.

"It's nice not to have to eat alone."

"Howard is unpredictable?" I said, trying to steer the conversation back to him.

She blew a short puff from her nose. "That's an understatement."

"What about your dad?" I said, taking a drink of full-fat milk. "Does he live nearby?"

"Ah, darlin', he passed away shortly after my mother did.

That's why I can afford this," she said, motioning to her tiny home. "I got half the inheritance money."

"And the other half," I prompted.

"Howard. But God knows what happened to all that money. I sure don't."

"Well, you must have a boyfriend," I said. Faye was very attractive, and she had her own house and business. In the nineteen-fifties, that was a big deal.

"Ah, nothing so sweet as that right now, honey."

It had gotten dark, so Faye switched on extra lights. "It's kind of late for y'to be walking home to an empty house. Do ya wanna stay here?"

"Really?" I was stunned and pleased at Faye's invitation to stay over.

"Unless you have school tomorrow? Or did ya drop out?"

Good idea. "I dropped out after moving again. I thought I'd get a job or something."

"You could work for me," Faye said. "It's not much for work, just sweeping and cleaning and the pay's minimal, but it's yours if ya want it."

A smile exploded over my face. "Yes, I want it."

I helped Faye clean the kitchen, doing an extra good job just to show her what kind of worker I'd be.

She opened a closet in the living room, pulling out a fold-away cot. "I'll push this out onto the back porch. It's fairly private and quiet. I had it screened in last year. You should sleep well out there."

Anything would be better than sleeping out in the wild on my own. Faye gave me a nightgown and an extra toothbrush.

"Do ya like to read before bed, Adeline? I have a few books y'could borrow. The porch light should be fine for reading."

"Sure, okay," I said. I didn't feel sleepy at all and a book might help.

"I like to read science fiction," Faye said with a stack of books in her arms. "Most people peg me for romance, but I prefer Ray Bradbury to Harlequin."

She was right. I would have pegged her for romance.

"I like science fiction, too," I said. Didn't I live real life science fiction? I had no choice but to like it.

"Okay, then. Good night, sleep tight," Faye said, leaving.

"Faye?" I called. She stopped. "I don't even know your last name."

"Johnson. Yours?"

"Savoy."

"Well, g'night, Adeline Savoy."

After slipping into the nightgown and brushing my teeth, I tucked myself into the new sheets on the cot and stared at the stars through the screen mesh walls.

This was my new home away from home, and I thought I would like it just fine.

FAYE DID WELL FOR A REASON. She worked hard. We were up early, had breakfast, cleaned the kitchen and then opened for business. Faye showed me her calendar for the day, booked solid until 4:00.

"And I thought you said people didn't book appointments."

"Ah, that was just an off day." Faye gave me instructions on her cleaning expectations, (high) and how to make customers feel welcome.

I became the official sweeper. After every haircut I swept the black and white checkered floor tiles while Faye wrote up a receipt and accepted her customer's cash, filing the bills into a drawer. I dusted the shelves, got coffee or tea for the ladies who wanted a beverage, and tidied the magazines. We closed for a lunch of tuna salad sandwiches and apple slices, and Faye lit up a cigarette.

I made a scene by fake coughing and fanning the smoke away from my face.

"You really should quit smoking, Faye."

Faye cocked an eyebrow. "But why? Everybody smokes."

"Because, you could get lung cancer or emphysema."

"Oh, my girl. You are a doomsdayer, aren't ya?"

The last appointment of the day was an elderly lady in for a perm. Faye chatted warmly with her like she did all her customers, and when she was done, I cleaned up the sink and perming tools (metal, fine-tooth comb with a pointed handle for parting hair, bottles and small bowls), while she took payment.

"Thank you, Mrs. Morgan," Faye said. "Come again."

"Oh, I will, Mrs. Johnson, I will."

Faye pretended not to notice the mistake in her name, and started humming.

"She called you *Mrs.* Johnson. That's weird."

Faye stopped humming. "Well, not really."

"You're married?"

"Divorced."

"Oh."

Faye blushed, embarrassed.

"It's no big deal, Faye. Divorce happens all the time."

"Maybe in Hollywood. It's the only reason I'm tolerated, I'm sure."

I couldn't imagine why any man would give up Faye, and I

almost said so, except a ruckus outside redirected our attention.

An old (to me) convertible car pulled up in front of the salon. It was loaded down with guys in leather jackets and upturned collars and girls in slim skirts with colorful scarves tied around their necks. I couldn't help but notice that every girl had short hair edged with pin curls.

And Howard sat in the front passenger seat, his arm around one of them.

Faye frowned. "He's so juvenile."

I watched through the window (again. I'd become a reverse peeper), as he high-fived his buddies and kissed the girl he had his arm around on the cheek.

I didn't like her.

The car roared off, and Howard, like a storm, came blasting through the door. He was the type of person whose presence took up the whole room, all the oxygen sucked out to make space. I felt light-headed.

"That was quite the entrance, Howard," Faye said. She seemed unimpressed and glanced at her watch. "Oh, no, I'm late. Adeline, darling, I'm late for my dentist appointment. Do y'mind closing up?"

"Sure, no problem."

"Just lock the door after me." Faye flipped the open sign over. We were now closed. Then she looked hard at Howard. "Maybe you should leave, too?"

Howard pulled a little brown paper bag out of his pocket and waved it in the air. "I'm gonna fix my truck. This here's a new spark plug."

"Your truck's outside." Faye could be very parental, I was finding.

"'Cept I'm hungry, Faye. Can ya fix me a sandwich, first?"

She flashed him a withering look. "I'm *late*, Howard. Make your own sandwich. And don't be bothering Adeline while you're at it, if you get what I'm saying."

Yes, very parental. I wasn't sure if it was over me or Howard. Maybe both.

Faye left and suddenly I found myself face to face with Howard. Alone.

"Hi," he said. "You probably already know this, but I'm Howard Walker."

I nodded. "I'm Adeline."

"Nice you meet ya, Adeline. Are y'working for Faye now?"

"Yes. And I'm kind of living here for awhile, too."

Howard tilted his head but didn't reply to this bit of info, then he said, "I'm going to eat something. You hungry?"

"Oh, no, I'm fine." My stomach was actually too busy doing somersaults to accept food at the moment. "I should finish up here."

Howard went to the kitchen and I worked like mad, sweeping and wiping and cleaning, hoping I could get finished before Howard left again. Just as I washed my hands in the sink and hung up my apron, Howard reappeared.

He leaned up against the wall as he stared at me, and dangled his truck keys in the air.

"You wanna go for a ride?"

FIVE

HOWARD QUICKLY replaced the spark plug then dropped the hood with a thud into place. You needed to work out for a year at the gym to manage the passenger door, it was so heavy, and it creaked as I opened it.

I settled in, my hand groping automatically for a seat belt but finding none. The seat was springy, the surface a hard, tan vinyl that was cracked and faded by the sun in places. Howard started it up, and the engine turned with a chug. He manhandled the ball ornament on top of a long rod that was the shift stick and moved it into reverse. We skidded off.

Sunset Boulevard in 1955 was a sight to behold, like the ultimate antique car show on a ribbon of gold lined with palm trees with fronds like long fingers, cheering in the wind. Car after car beaded by, all with smooth, jolly, rounded lines, shiny chrome bumpers and big circular headlights. I felt like I was on a movie set, the leading lady with a scarf around coifed hair, glamorous in dark sunglasses, smiling from a '55 Ford convertible.

Except that I was in a loud, old-for-the-times, truck, with no scarf or sunglasses.

But, I did have my leading man. I couldn't help sneaking glances at Howard's profile. His strong jaw was cleanly shaved. His dirty blond hair was slicked back with just the right amount of sideburns. A pack of cigarettes bulged from the cuff of his T-shirt where it was rolled up and his shifting arm flexed nicely with every gear shift. His left hand rested casually on top of an oversized steering wheel, and the whole scene was just hot, hot, hot.

"What kind of truck is this?" I said over the rumble of the engine.

" '39 Chevy."

"Nice."

"She's a temperamental thing. Just like a woman."

"Hey. That's very stereotypical," I said.

Howard glanced at me and grinned. "You denying it?"

I smiled back. "No."

Howard turned off Sunset toward the hills with the Hollywood sign.

"Do you have a job, Howard?"

"Work ebbs and flows. I'm a musician."

Really? "Faye never mentioned that."

"That's because Faye doesn't consider music a real job. Or at least she doesn't think that I can make it one."

"A music career can be unpredictable."

"Life is unpredictable, Adeline. You gotta take risks sometimes or y'might as well just lie down and die. Get it over with."

"Maybe you should get into acting," I said. "You do look a bit like James Dean."

"Rats. I hate it when people say that. That's exactly why I chose music over acting. They don't need another James Dean. They already have one."

Not for long. I looked it up. He will die on September 30th. I wondered how Howard would take the news when he hears it. "I'm sorry."

"No, it's not your fault. I know I resemble the guy. I think I'm going to get Faye to dye my hair darker, like Dean Martin."

We pulled into a lookout with a view of the Hollywood valley. A couple of kids in the car next to us were making out. I hoped Howard didn't have any ideas. I wasn't ready to let our relationship go that far yet.

Especially since we weren't in a relationship.

Howard motioned for me to follow him out of the truck. We leaned up against the front bumper watching as the street-lights in the valley below started to pop on.

Howard shoved his fists in his pockets. "How old are you, anyway?"

"Eighteen." It just slipped out. I couldn't believe I'd just lied about my age.

"Eighteen," Howard said, like he was rolling the number around in his mouth. "Are you sure about that?"

It was my ponytail. It made me look too young. "I think I know my own age," I insisted.

"Well, then, would you like a beer?" Howard stepped over to the side of his truck and reached in to open a cooler.

"Eighteen's not drinking age," I said. Besides I hated the taste of beer. I shook my head.

"Who's gonna tell?" Howard had a can opener on his key chain and used it to remove the cap off the bottle. He took a swig, then eyed me with a tilt of his head. "I don't really like girls who drink beer, anyway. Not very attractive."

Howard returned to the front bumper, leaning in a few inches closer than before. "How about a smoke?" he said as he lit one for himself. I shook my head again. I must look like such a baby to him but I couldn't very well accept after the lecture I gave Faye.

"You're a good girl, eh?"

"What's that supposed to mean?"

He laughed. "Ah, nothing."

Thinking of the girl in the car when Howard arrived at Faye's, I asked, "Do you have a girlfriend?"

"Nah."

"Who was that girl you were with in the car, then?"

"Oh her, that was Penny. She's just a pal."

"She looked to be more than a *pal* to me."

"Cuz I kissed her goodbye? We're just friendly. Why, are y'jealous?"

How could I admit to that? I just met the guy and already I was coming off as pushy and needy. "No, no. Of course not. Just curious."

I thought I'd try another tactic. "Do you play guitar?"

"Yup. Just got myself a beautiful Gibson. It ain't brand new, but she plays like a charm."

"Do you write your own songs, too, then?"

"Sometimes." Howard dropped his cigarette, scrubbing it out with his boot and tossed his empty bottle in the back of his truck. "We should go."

"So, what do you do when you're not making music?" I said as I hopped back into his truck. I couldn't help but notice that something was keeping Howard fit.

"Ah, there's always lots to do in the valley. Mostly farm stuff. I pick up odd jobs."

The radio cracked with poor reception and Howard turned it off. He tapped his fingers on his thigh and started humming while I snuck peeks at his profile, not wanting to look like the infatuated schoolgirl that I was.

Howard cranked the gangly steering wheel to make the turn onto Faye's street.

"I gotta gig tomorrow, if ya wanna come?" he said.

Was he asking me out? Or just being friendly? Yeah, he was just being friendly. Probably. But, I'd take any opportunity to see him again.

"I have to be at sound check at three o'clock."

"I work until 4:30."

"Ah, Faye will let ya go. I'll pick y'up at two."

Howard stopped at the front of Faye's salon. I could see lights on at the back. I hoped that Faye hadn't worried about me when she got home from the dentist and found I was gone.

I pushed the bulky truck door open and stepped out. "Thanks, Howard that was fun. See you tomorrow."

"Sure thing, sugar." Howard winked and drove off into the sunset.

SIX

NEEDLESS TO SAY, Faye wasn't too thrilled about the fact that I'd gone driving with her brother or that he'd asked me out. Sort of.

"He's too old for ya."

"But you just said he was really immature for his age. Doesn't that make him, like, younger?"

"Like younger what? Girls?"

That was not what I meant but Faye had her head in the fridge, searching for supper items, so I didn't bother trying to explain.

"Every time Howard eats here, he leaves a big mess." Her voice echoed from the cavern of the open refrigerator.

Faye put a carton of eggs, a block of cheese and a bunch of green onions on the counter. I was guessing omelets?

"I don't pretend to know ya, Adeline, but I know my brother. You seem like a sweet girl, and let's just say, Howard has broken more than a few hearts."

Maybe. But I could be different. There was always the girl that changed the bad boy for good, right? I would be that girl.

Faye wouldn't get it, so I decided it would be in my best interest to change the subject.

"I started reading *Fahrenheit 451* last night. It's pretty interesting." And kind of strange. I ran my fingers across the cover. Blue background with a man dressed in a futuristic suit made of what looked like pages ripped from a book. A fire licked the guy's feet like he was a Salem witch, and he had his hand covering his face as his suit burned.

The price of thirty-five cents was stamped on the top left hand corner. I put the book down and began to set the table.

"It's a warning about the future," Faye said as she flipped the first omelets. "Censorship and such. Can't imagine a world without books."

We still had books in the future, though Faye would be surprised at what we read them on.

I WOKE EARLY the next day, excited for my upcoming date with Howard. I imagined him performing on some stage strumming his guitar, all hot and handsome with girls fainting, and me sitting there watching, as his eyes singled me out.

Faye noticed my cheerful mood, and then I realized I hadn't even asked for the time off. And I would wager a bet that she wouldn't want to give it to me if she knew what it was for.

But I didn't want to lie to her. I respected Faye too much for that, and look at all she was doing for me. I couldn't jeopardize that. I'd just have to take my chances.

"Faye?" She was setting out the color products for our first customer who was due to arrive any minute.

"Howard said I could go to his gig... with him today? To see how they set up for a concert?" I thought it best *not* to make it about seeing Howard specifically. "Is it all right if I take some of the afternoon off? He said he'd pick me up."

"Oh sweet Adeline! Why do y'not heed my warnings?"

Because I'm sixteen and hopelessly in love?

"You know." Her head dropped to the side, clearly pitying me. "He may not show. He's famous for breaking promises."

I was sure he'd show. "If he doesn't show, I'll just keep working, and we won't have to talk about it."

"Okay. But just so ya know, I'm agreeing against my better judgment." The bell over the door rang. Faye's first appointment had arrived.

I couldn't help but check the clock on the wall. Repeatedly.

"A watched pot never boils," Faye finally said, exasperated.

Finally, two o'clock rolled around. I removed my apron and checked my hair. "Faye, do you think I could borrow a lipstick?"

Faye took a deep breath. I wasn't sure if she was annoyed because I asked to use her make up or because I wanted to wear lipstick for her brother.

"Fine, pick whatever one you like." Faye kept a selection in the drawer by the mirror in the salon. She always wanted to look "fresh and ready for anything."

I opted for *Frosted Pink*. I checked my reflection in the circular mirror on the wall. Faye had kept me clothed in fashionable skirts and blouses and I looked pretty good.

I checked the time again. Twelve minutes after two. Howard was late. Was Faye right? Would he stand me up?

Two more minutes. Five more minutes. Anxiety twisted and turned in my gut. Then anger. The embers in my belly started to burn. Would he really do this to me? Ask me to go out and then not pick me up, without phoning or anything? As each second ticked by, I could feel my breath come heavier, puffing like a dragon through my nose.

Half past two.

Faye had been right. I was such a sucker.

Then I heard the loud familiar rumble of his truck, but I was already so mad at him for being late, I could barely muster a smile.

I shouldn't let myself get wound up. It wasn't good for me. I felt dizzy.

Oh, no. I thought that Howard had stood me up, but now I knew I would be standing him up instead. "Faye," I called as I ran to the back door of the salon. "Tell Howard I'm sorry."

I made it to the back porch before I disappeared.

SEVEN

I'D TOTALLY FORGOTTEN about the soccer game. I was on the ground, curled in a ball, moaning. Not because Paul and the other oaf had hurt me, but because I'd made myself miss my date with Howard Walker! I was so mad at myself! Maybe if I got mad enough, I'd travel right back there. I lay on my back, trying to keep my anger level up, but the monster had resided. Traveling back to the present was exhausting, and fatigue sapped all the steam out of my anger, leaving me to mellow in disappointment instead.

The boys had scrimmaged back to the center line. I was left heaving on the ground. No one even came over to see if I was okay.

After a few moments I got up and brushed grass off my ugly gym clothes. I walked off the field dazed like a drunkard, heading straight for the changing rooms, ten minutes before the end of class. Either the teacher didn't notice or didn't care.

After school I jostled my way through the crowds going directly to the bus stop, hoping to avoid encountering anyone I knew. Of course, Marco spotted me and rolled up on his skateboard.

"So, how was your first day?"

Ah, it sucked? I tried to remember what had actually happened on this day. I just shrugged in response.

"You have grass in your hair," Marco said. "I take it, not so well?"

He started picking the grass out of my hair and I let him. He actually smelled really good, sort of woodsy, which surprised me for some reason and his close proximity was kind of comforting. Brotherly.

"Tomorrow you're in my Social Studies class," he said. "I'll save you a seat."

"Thanks."

I saw another skater ride by with a familiar profile. It took a few moments for recognition to click in. That was Candice's boyfriend, and it triggered the memory of the fight that I'd witnessed.

"Hey, Marco, about your sister's boyfriend?"

"Dan Highland?" Marco's eyes darted to the stairwell behind him. Dan Highland had climbed the steps and was poised at the top to do some crazy jump thing. "What about him?"

"Is he okay?"

"Okay, how?"

"Do you like him?"

Marco shrugged. "He's not my favorite one, but Candace will move on to a new guy soon enough. She changes boyfriends with the cycle of the moon. I've honestly lost count."

He did a little skateboard flip thing. He obviously had more energy than I did.

"I'm going to hang back to skate," he said. "You okay riding with Bluebell?"

"Sure, that's fine."

He smiled and then rolled back to the stairwell.

I turned and found Bluebell waiting for me.

"You look tired, Ad." Bluebell wrinkled her forehead. I wondered if it hurt her eyebrow piercing to do that. "You have dark rings around your eyes."

"Yeah, I'm kind of zonked," I said, looking away. I remembered, now, how I'd embarrassed her in the hall before our choir class. She seemed to have forgotten it.

"Did you make any new friends?" she asked.

Well, I did, if you counted Howard, but I shook my head.

"This school can take *forev* to break into." Bluebell shifted her weight on her brace. "I've lived here my whole life and I'm still not in."

Not comforting, actually.

This time I waited for her to shuffle to the bus doors when it arrived, letting her go first.

I dragged my feet walking from the bus stop to my house. Traveling to the future was much more exhausting than going to the past for some reason. I couldn't wait to crawl into my bed for a much needed nap. I totally planned to dream about Howard.

The door was unlocked, which meant Dad was home.

I could hear him in the living room. "I'm telling you, it wasn't me..."

Then, a woman's voice responding, "Take it up with the judge, Mr. Clark."

Dad was delivering lines with someone. I hoped it wasn't that Spring lady from the Shop & Save. "Dad, I'm home."

"Adeline, hello. Wow, is it that time already?"

It wasn't Spring. This time it was a red head. Let me guess, *Autumn?*

"Adeline, this is, January, from my acting class."

January? Oh, brother. What was with the season themes?

"Hello," I forced myself to say.

"January's offered to make us dinner tonight. That will be a nice treat, won't it?"

"I can whip up a mean Chicken Korma," January said. "Not too hot, just nice."

I tried to picture January in our kitchen. With my dad. Could she cook? Then I had this weird vision of Faye cooking in our kitchen. She made the kind of meals Dad really liked, good old-fashioned meat and potatoes. Dad didn't suit these women he was hanging out with at the acting school.

He suited Faye.

"Sounds great," I said wearily, heading straight for my room.

I peeled off my clothes and let myself daydream about Faye living with us. I liked Faye. She wasn't my mother, but I could tell she really cared about me. No woman had treated me with such maternal kindness since my mom. Not Janice from Cambridge, not any of my neighbors or teachers, and certainly none of the women my dad seemed to like.

I slipped in between my cool cotton sheets in just my underclothes. I was sleeping before my head hit the pillow.

. . .

THE REST of the week went off without a hitch. Marco was in both my Social Studies and History classes, we met up with Bluebell and the two Bs (Bing and Bong) for lunch, Paul from Gym still called me the Girl in the Brown Shirt (like I knew he would), and I never left the twenty-first century.

I hugged my books as Bluebell and I rode the bus home on Friday.

Bluebell's eye ring inched up as she looked over at me. "Do you want to come over?"

"Over?"

"Yeah, to my house. Hang out."

I tried to hide the surprise I felt, keeping my expression blank. I didn't usually get invited places. It didn't help that I wasn't the friendliest of people, but being a loner suited my unique situation.

"Uh, I don't know."

Bluebell's eyes closed and she shuddered. "It's fine. I just thought..."

"Okay." I heard myself say. Bluebell's eyes sprung open. I didn't know who was more surprised by my response, me or her?

I texted dad to let him know (I was sure he'd be thrilled to hear I had made a friend), and stayed on the bus when it rattled to a stop where I usually got off. The bus continued on from there up the hill not far from the lookout Howard had taken me to, and into a posh, gated neighborhood. It stopped right in front of a house. No, not a house, a mansion. A gigantic wood and stone affair pushed back from the road with an iron gate in front.

"This is my stop," Bluebell said.

I followed her as she limped off. A man at the gate drove us up the long snaky driveway in a pimped up golf cart.

"You live *here*?" I gawked at a grand three-storey structure. It had shiny, red Spanish tiles on the roof, and a veranda with black, wrought iron railings off every window. Vines crawled up the walls and stone fountains with elaborate statues of mystical creatures shot water high into the air.

Let's just say I was a little stunned. I'd never guessed that Bluebell lived in such wealth. She certainly didn't come off as a rich snob.

"Wow, Bluebell."

"I know. It's ostentatious."

We exited the cart and entered through two heavy, tall, wooden front doors that opened up into a vast foyer. A woman dressed in a powder blue, cotton smock with a white apron tied around her waist skittered over to us.

"Welcome home, Miss Bluebell," she said with a thick Spanish accent. "Did you have a good day?"

"*Si, Senorita*," Bluebell said. "And this is my friend, Adeline."

Senorita's dark, dewy eyes widened when they settled on me. I got the feeling that Bluebell didn't bring friends home that often.

She quickly recovered with a big smile and took both of our backpacks, hiding them in a concealed closet under the stairwell.

I followed Bluebell into an enormous kitchen, vast like a restaurant, full of stainless steel appliances and countertops so shiny I could easily see my reflection.

"Are you hungry?" Bluebell asked.

"A little."

She opened a refrigerator the size of my walk-in closet and pulled out a tray already prepared. Cheese, crackers, grapes, and chocolates.

"How?" I started.

"Senorita Maria always has something ready for me after school. I tell her not to, I can get it myself, but she insists. Do you mind taking the juice?"

We sat outside on a deck off the kitchen that had a view of the city, and a kidney shaped pool off to the side. I let out a long breath. So this was how the other half lived.

"Have you lived here a long time?" I reached for a cracker and a slice of cheese.

"Most my life. My dad wants to upgrade to Beverly Hills, but he and my mom decided to wait until I've finished school." She glanced at her withered leg. "No sense exposing me to a whole new group of kids."

I couldn't miss the slight sarcasm that seeped through in her tone of voice.

"What does your dad do?"

"He's an executive at MGM."

A big movie studio. That explained the wealth, I guess. "So, do you get to meet the big stars?"

Bluebell shrugged. "Sometimes. My dad doesn't really like me to hang around him."

"Why not?"

"Because of this." She pointed to her leg.

"Really?" That seemed harsh.

"Yeah, you know, it's very important to be perfect in Hollywood, in case you haven't noticed."

"Well," I said popping a grape into my mouth. "You can't really miss it."

"Especially when you're not perfect, which obviously I'm not."

"Bluebell, nobody is perfect."

"Tell that to my dad. At any rate, he doesn't like me hanging around. I'm kind of a well kept secret."

That sucked. I didn't know what to say, either. I pushed a chocolate in my mouth and made "um" noises.

"What about your dad?" Bluebell asked.

"He wants to be an actor."

"Oh no. Not another one."

"That's why we moved here from Cambridge. He'd die to meet your dad, I bet."

"I bet," Bluebell said, but didn't offer to make the introduction.

We put the dishes into the dishwasher and Bluebell took me to her room, which was upstairs. It took a while, with how she had to drag her leg brace up one step at a time. I was surprised she didn't have her own elevator or something.

"Sorry," she said. "I know you don't like to move slowly."

"No, Bluebell, I don't mind. I'm sorry for being a jerk the other day."

"Ah, that's okay. It was your first day. Stressful. I get it."

All along the wall of the stairwell were framed pictures of a good-looking well-dressed man with various movie stars: Harrison Ford, Will Smith, Julia Roberts.

"Is that your dad?" I asked.

"Yeah." She stopped to point at a petite, dark-haired woman dressed in an expensive looking ball gown. "That's my mother."

"She's beautiful."

"Of course she is."

Her bedroom was the first door to the right at the top of the stairs. By now I'd expected something large and ornate filled with everything a person could want. I wasn't wrong.

"Cool room," I said, noting all the toys, dolls, child-sized dollhouse, books. Lots of books, a practical library, and a cozy looking chair to read by. The only incongruent thing was the collection of canes and braces propped up in one corner.

Bluebell saw me staring.

"My physiotherapist comes here once a week for my treatment. Wouldn't want the paparazzi catching John Seymour's crippled daughter going to a treatment center."

Wow. She was angrier at her father than I was at mine. And here I thought we didn't have anything in common.

We sat on her bed and I picked up a stuffed toy dog. Petting it made me feel better somehow. "Is Bluebell a nickname?"

"Nope. I wouldn't be so lucky. If you stick around Hollywood long enough you'll discover that no one has a normal name, especially the kids of famous/near famous people."

"Yeah, that I've noticed." Spring and January came to mind.

"So," Bluebell said, looking at me. "Now you know why I don't have many friends. What's your excuse?"

The muscles in my shoulders tensed defensively. "I have friends."

"Marco doesn't count."

"Why?"

"Because he's friends with everybody."

That was true, I realized. For some reason I found that awareness unsettling. I kind of like the idea that Marco had found something in me that he thought was special. I knew it was vain thinking on my part, but I'd thought he had a little crush on me. And even though I didn't return the feelings, I still liked the thought that he liked me.

I could be so stupid. He was just being friendly, because that was how he was.

"Ad?"

"You know what *Blue,* I don't like it when you shorten my name."

"Whoa, okay. *Adeline,* your many friends?

"Oh, yeah, so what? I don't need a lot of friends. You can only know so many people well. More than that and you're just playing with them."

Bluebell scoffed. "You really believe that?"

I didn't know. I thought it sounded good. It felt like Bluebell could see right through me, and I didn't like that.

"Why, do you care?" I asked. "Why work so hard at trying to be my friend? And don't tell me you feel sorry for me!"

"Why would *I* feel sorry for *you?* I don't even feel sorry for myself."

That was true. Bluebell never gave off that pity-me vibe.

"But you know what they say," she added. "If you want a friend, you have to be a friend."

I knew that saying. I just didn't know if I wanted any friends. They could be so nosy and annoying and pushy.

EIGHT

THE NEXT DAY Marco asked if I wanted to go with him to the beach. I thought about what Bluebell had said about being friendly if I wanted friends, so I told him yes, but I reminded him I didn't surf.

"Is Bluebell coming?" I asked when we got to the metro bus station. Now that I officially had two friends, I wanted to know where she was. (Actually, I had three friends if I counted Faye. I didn't count Howard. He was in a different, juicier category.)

"Nope."

"How come?"

"I didn't ask her."

Why not? Was this an attempt by him to be alone with me? If it was, should I be bothered by this?

Strangely, I wasn't.

Besides, I needed to smack myself. Marco was friends with *everyone*.

"Bluebell doesn't like the beach," Marco explained. "It's

hard for her to navigate the sand with her brace, otherwise I would have."

And now I had confirmation. I wasn't anything special. As Bluebell would say, "That's tote fine."

"How are you going to surf without a surfboard?" I'd just clued in that he wasn't carrying one.

"Too big to bring on the bus. You can rent them there. They're not as good as my own, but it does in a pinch. I get my license next year, then I can strap my board to the top of my mom's car."

The 704 took us all the way down Santa Monica Boulevard to the ocean. The beach was wide and long with people scattered here and there, not as busy as I'd imagined, though it was September which meant less tourism. From where we landed, the Ferris wheel on the Santa Monica pier was a small ring in the distance.

The sun still had enough scorch in it to heat up the sand and when I took my flip-flops off, I quickly stepped onto my towel. The wind blew my hair around my face even though I'd tied it back before we left, and I brushed loose strands behind my ears. I breathed in the salty ocean air and felt myself relax.

Sitting down, I loosened the top buttons of my fifties-style high-waist shorts. My T-shirt hung loosely over it, so you couldn't really see them. Not that anyone around here would care.

I ran my fingers through the sand. It felt odd to me that it was mid September and still warm enough to go swimming. Back in Cambridge we'd be pulling out snow gear, just in case.

Marco sat beside me. "It's beautiful, isn't it?"

I nodded.

He continued, "I love the ocean. The salt in my nose, the

loud roar of the waves in my ears, the mightiness of it all. How on one hand it offers food and sustenance and a way to travel the world, and on the other, it has the power to take your life, just like that."

I agreed. "It is amazing."

"It must be so different from Cambridge."

"Oh yeah. I was just thinking that."

"Do you miss it there?"

I squinted in the glare of the sun off the ocean. "Sometimes."

"What do you miss the most?"

That was a hard question to answer, but it wasn't because I didn't know. "My mother. Or rather the memories of my mother."

Marco's eyes softened. "Did she die?"

I nodded. "When I was ten. She had breast cancer."

"I'm sorry to hear that."

I cocked my head to look at him. I hated when people simply said, I'm sorry, like it was their fault, and then I'd have to comfort them in a backward way. But I couldn't fault him for being sorry to hear it. It was bad news.

"What about friends?" he probed. "Did you leave a boyfriend behind?"

I didn't really have friends, a fact that had been already well established by Bluebell. I was naturally a loner. I didn't mind solitude. Plus, with my *condition*, it just seemed better to keep my life as simple and as drama free as possible.

"Are you asking me if I have a boyfriend?"

"I guess I am."

The breeze blew strands of my hair across my face, and I

was glad Marco couldn't see my eyes, because I knew I was about to lie to him. "Sort of."

"You sort of have a boyfriend?"

"It's complicated. It's kind of long distance."

"Oh, yeah. Those kinds are tough."

"How would you know?"

"I have two older sisters, remember? They cry a lot. What's his name?"

"Who?"

"Your sort of boyfriend."

Oh. "Howard?"

"You're not sure? Is his name Howard or isn't it?"

"Yes, it is, now if you don't mind, I'd rather not talk about it."

"Sure. I'm going to go rent a board." Marco sprung up and sprinted to the rental stand. He was in bare feet, and the sand got hot quickly. He started jumping and running on his toes, making me laugh.

When he got back he jumped onto his towel. "Man, that's hot for this time of year." He did a little bird dance. "I just about burned my feet off."

I laughed. "You look like an idiot."

"Thank you. So, are you coming in?"

"I didn't wear my suit."

"You told me you weren't surfing, not that you weren't swimming. Don't tell me you don't swim?"

"I swim." I took lessons when I was younger, before my life as a time traveler started. "I just didn't feel like it today."

Marco relented. "Okay. Next time, though. Next time you go in with me."

He was so bossy.

I watched him surf and I had to admit, it was a nice way to spend an afternoon. Marco was a good surfer, and he impressed me with how he managed the waves. I leaned back on my elbows and let the sun massage all my worries away. This California lifestyle could work for me.

I must've dozed off because next thing I knew I was experiencing Chinese water torture. I sprung up onto my elbows and stared into Marco's wet, smiling face. Drops of water dripped from the tips of his curls onto me.

"Hey!"

"Hey, what?" He grabbed his towel and I admit to sneaking glances at his fit form as he dried off. "I'm starved," he said as he pulled his T-shirt over his head.

We grabbed a burger to go before heading home.

"That was a nice time, Marco." I unwrapped my burger, keeping the napkin tight to soak up the grease. "Thanks for taking me."

"You're welcome. We'll do it again soon."

It was a comfortable ride home. When we got to my house, Marco said "It's still early. Do you want to come over?"

We'd already spent most of the day together, and you know what they say about too much of a good thing. "I don't think so. I should spend some time with my dad."

"Oh, okay."

But just as Marco was about to leave, my dad drove in.

And he had a passenger.

"Hi, Adeline," he called out to me when he exited the car. "Molly's going to help me get ready for my audition Monday."

Well, at least this one had a semi-normal name, and she was the first blonde one. Like my mom. Except taller and younger, with lips that looked like a blowfish.

Suddenly, home was the last place I wanted to be.

Marco and I watched as my dad unlocked the front door with his key. Obviously, this was hilarious because the blonde giggled through it.

"I'll be at Marco's," I called out, but I didn't think Dad even heard me.

"You don't like it when he brings girls home, do you?"

"I don't care what my dad does."

"Yes, you do."

This guy knew how to push my buttons. "You know, Marco, you think you know me, but you don't."

"It's not unusual for teenagers to be uncomfortable when their single parent brings home friends of the opposite sex. *This* I know from experience."

"Your mom brings guys home?" I said, unbelieving.

"There's no shame in being lonely. And at least she usually picks decent guys."

"So, why isn't she with someone?"

"It's tough to find a guy who's interested in an instant family. Four kids is a lot to take on. And Mom doesn't want to rush into anything because of us kids, you know, mess with our little worlds."

"But what about my little world?" I whined. "Look at how my dad is messing with me."

"Do any of the girls ever stay over?"

"No! They're just acting friends."

"So what's wrong with your little world then?"

"For one thing, Dad moved me from Cambridge to play act and even though he said we'd spend a lot more time together because he wouldn't be stuck in an office all day, we don't."

"Okay. Now we're getting somewhere."

"Are you *analyzing* me?" I crossed my arms, feeling justifiably indignant.

"Look, I don't think we should continue this conversation out here. Everyone in the block can hear us."

That startled me. Did my dad just hear what I'd said? I turned to our house and let out a breath. Michael Bublé tunes from our living room blocked our conversation.

I fudged. I didn't really want to go with Marco and let him tell me all the things that were wrong with me, but I didn't want to go home either. Dad and I plus strange woman did not a comfortable evening make.

Marco's house was full of activity. His little sister watched cartoons in the living room; the sister I saw with the angry boyfriend in the hallway, Candice, was talking on the phone; and another teen girl, I presumed to be the third sister, hauled a basket of laundry upstairs.

"Don't get sand everywhere, Marco," she shouted as she passed us. "I just vacuumed."

"That was Lucy." Marco surprised me by leading me to his room. He must've noted the look on my face because he added, "It's the only place in the house we'll get privacy."

"Your mom won't mind?"

"Nah, besides, she's at work."

Marco's room was tidy but not neat-freak clean like I'd expected. A desk and chair were in the corner and a laptop sat opened on top. He had posters of surfers on the wall, and one of the map of the world, only upside down. At least the map was upside down. The writing was still upside up.

"It's upside down," I stated the obvious.

"Why do you say that?"

"Well, Canada and the United States are at the bottom, and Australia is at the top."

"Who says, North America is at the top? That's strictly an American way to see things. Out in space there is no up and down. The world is a sphere, suspended in infinite space."

"I know that, but it's weird."

"I like it. I like to see things from different perspectives, look at life from outside of the box."

Marco threw his towel into his closet, gesturing to me to sit on his desk chair. He picked up his guitar and sat on the bed.

"Are you any good?" I said, wondering how he would compare to Howard, assuming I'd ever stick around long enough in the fifties to hear Howard play at some point.

"I'm not a rock star. I won't make a living at it, if that's what you mean."

"So why do you play?"

"Just for fun, Adeline. Have you heard of it? Doing things for fun?"

"You're such a smart aleck." I put my feet up on his bed, crossing them at the ankles.

"Well?" he said.

"Well, what?"

"What do you do for fun, Adeline Savoy?"

"I don't know."

He pushed his hair out of his eyes and looked to the ceiling like he was thinking. His eyes were a very warm brown in this light. His biceps flexed nicely as he air strummed his guitar.

Oh, stop it, Adeline. He was a pain in the neck.

"I'll give you an example of what I'm talking about. Take me, for instance. I like to surf for fun, play guitar for fun, bug my sisters for fun—"

"I believe that," I scoffed.

"I bake chocolate cookies for fun."

"You bake?" I asked.

"Just chocolate cookies, but I nail it. I'll bake you some, sometime.

The way his warm eyes latched on to mine, challenging yet compassionate—it was weird and disconcerting.

"So? What's your list?" he pressed.

It was awful. I couldn't think of anything. Was I that boring? A fun-less, boring time traveler? Hey, I time traveled. That was interesting. But I didn't do it for fun, so that didn't count. I had to do something for fun. I wasn't dead, was I? Then I thought of something.

"I read science fiction for fun." Even though I had only started that recently at Faye's.

"Really? What do you read?"

"At the moment I'm reading Ray Bradbury."

"Which one?"

"What? You don't believe me? You think I'm making it up?"

"No. I read science fiction, too. I've read most of Bradbury's work. I just wondered which one."

"Fine. It's *Fahrenheit 451*—and I'm not finished with it yet, so don't give it away."

A stony silence filled the room. Why was it that we always ended up fighting? Then, Marco started playing his guitar, finger picking style. He was pretty good.

Marco was good at a lot of things.

I was too antsy to just sit there. I got up to look out his window. I passed a small framed black and white photo of a man playing a fat guitar and paused to look.

"Who's this?"

"My grandpa. Carlos Rodriguez. He was a jazz guitarist, got quite popular in California in his day. He was known as Carl Rodney, but he never broke out. He blamed the onslaught of Rock and Roll."

"Are you guys close?"

"He died before I was born. I wish I could've met him though. He emigrated from Mexico in 1947 with his family, and worked on a farm his whole life. Married my grandmother. They had a bunch of kids and then he died. My grandmother remarried, but legend has it that she never got over Carlos. When her second husband died, she put her first set of wedding rings back on. They buried her with them on.

"Really?"

"It's what she wanted."

"That's so romantic."

Marco put his guitar down. "In a tragic sort of way."

I pushed the spaceship print curtains out of the way and looked down at the lower level windows of my house. Yeah, he could see into my room. Just part way, but still. I'd have to make a point of changing against the far wall.

I could see into the living room a bit, too. Shadows. Dad and the new chick were dancing. Was that part of their audition? I doubted it.

I felt a lump form in my throat and my eyes grew scratchy. Marco must've sensed something was wrong (of course, Marco was good at everything) because the next thing I knew he was standing beside me at the window.

"My last clear memory of my mother is my fifth birthday." My words came out all tight and gargled. "She baked me a chocolate cake and let me lick the bowl. I remember her laughing and staring at me with eyes full of love as she wiped the batter off my cheeks."

"Sounds like she was a wonderful mother."

My eyes prickled with the threat of tears. "I miss her," I whispered.

"I know," he said softly. "That's what really bugs you about your dad's friends. You can't picture any of them filling the role of your mother and you're afraid your dad will fall for one of them."

I started sobbing. I hated Marco in that moment for being right. He was always right.

I covered my face with my hair. It was bad enough I was crying, but to add a red blotchy face to that was a double whammy.

Then I felt his arms around me. I wanted to push him away, but it just felt too good to be held. I let him hold me as I slobbered on his shoulders.

He didn't say "don't cry", or "everything will be all right". He just let me cry.

When the worst was over, I pulled away. "Do you have a tissue?" It came out in little hiccups.

Marco presented one like a magician. I blew my nose in a most unattractive manner and sadly caught a glimpse of myself in Marco's mirror. Yikes. My face was all blotchy and my nose was as red as Rudolph's.

"I think I'll go home now," I said feeling embarrassed. Marco just nodded but his eyes never faltered as they followed me to the door.

Despite my hideous appearance there seemed to be a moment between us. A thread of something important, tying us together. I shivered with the shot of electricity that pulsed through me.

I was being stupid. Marco was just being his friendly self, and besides, I couldn't forget about how I felt about Howard.

I forced a smile. "I can find my way out."

NINE

I SLIPPED IN QUIETLY, peeking in on my dad and his new "friend." Michael Bublé had led to a bottle of white wine being opened up and shared.

Blah.

In my room I crawled into bed, even though it was barely dusk and stared at the ceiling. I couldn't help comparing the blond in the living room (who seemed like another Barbie doll enamored with the 90028 zip code) with Faye. Faye was a strong independent woman who made something of her life even with a lot of strikes against her. Both parents and a husband were gone.

She would be perfect for Dad. And for me. Why was she born in the wrong decade?

Or maybe I was the one born at the wrong time? I should feel at home in the twenty-first century, but I didn't really fit in. I was way more comfortable living with Faye and crushing on Howard, than I was here with my own dad.

Or with Marco. I recalled the sensation of Marco with his

arms around me. In that instant I'd felt safe and cared for and though I hated that I was such a freaking billboard with my emotions, I appreciated the comfort of his hug. But did I feel anything else? Was it thrilling?

There was no denying that Marco was cute. Still, that boy frustrated me. He was too smart, too right, too good. His life was all planned out and predictable. (Hello, he planned on going to UC to study psychology. He was getting lots of practice psychoanalyzing me.)

Unlike Howard, who was older (didn't that make him wiser?) and took life one day at a time. I was attracted to his devil-may-care attitude, and he was definitely very easy to look at.

What would it feel like if Howard put his arms around me? Even in my imagination, the thought excited me. I wondered if I'd ever get to find out for sure.

Hunger kept me from hiding out in my room. I soft-shoed my way to the kitchen and glanced into the living room, where Dad and the blonde were sitting on the couch. Close. Very close.

They were kissing.

My stomach fell to my feet and a flush of anger overwhelmed me. "Dad!"

He pulled out of their lip-suck and ran a hand through his hair like that would erase the image of what I'd just seen from the back of my eyeballs.

"Adeline, oh, I didn't know you had come home."

Duh.

"Molly and I were just talking about supper plans. We thought we'd order Chinese. How's that sound?"

Like I was going to stick around and eat dinner with them. "Sounds fine," I said through clenched teeth.

I went to my room and slammed the door. The next moment, Dad was inside with me.

"Don't you slam the door on me, Adeline!"

I crossed my arms and stared him down. "Why do you keep bringing women home, Dad?"

Dad closed my door. Lowering his voice, he said, "I don't bring women home. I bring friends."

I huffed.

"Why are you being so rude, anyway, Adeline? I never raised you like that."

"*You* never raised me, Dad. Isn't that the problem? I thought our move to Hollywood was supposed to be a new start for *us*? So far, it's just been a new start for you!"

I couldn't stay here. I pushed past Dad, leaving my room.

"Adeline!"

I ran out the front door, my heart beating against my ribs. I hated my dad!

By the time I made it to our front patio, I was hit with a wave of dizziness and bright light. I was back in 1955 amid the weeds and open space. Relieved to finally be back, I wiped away a stray angry tear and sprinted toward Faye's place.

I was out of breath when I knocked on the side door of the house. It was after hours and the salon was closed.

Faye was surprised to see me. "Adeline? Come in."

Now that I was there, I was nervous. I had my fifties shorts on but my shirt didn't really fit in. Faye didn't seem to notice my clothes.

"Are y'crying?" she said. I sat down on the sofa.

"Oh, it's nothing." I wiped the moisture from my eyes and

calmed my breath. Faye went to the kitchen and returned with a glass of water.

"It's never nothing, darling," she said as she handed it to me.

"It's my dad. He has a girlfriend." I gulped the water down. "I guess I shouldn't be so surprised, but it's just that I've never seen him with anyone other than my mother before."

Faye sat beside me and put an arm around me. "My dad died soon after my mother so I didn't have to go through seeing him with someone else, but honey, I can't imagine it. It must be hard."

She was *so* understanding. Why couldn't Dad meet someone like Faye?

"But," she continued, "just because he upset ya, it's not a good reason to run away."

"I didn't run..." I started, but then again, I did run away, I just didn't mean to come here. "Anyway, it doesn't matter. He's traveling again." Actually, I was the one traveling all the time. It was hard to keep it straight, sometimes.

"Well, y'can always stay with me, okay? Any time ya need a place."

"Oh, Faye." I felt the tears coming again. She pulled me into a big hug and it was the second time in one day I slobbered on someone's shoulder.

"You must be hungry," Faye said. I was. "I'll fix us something to eat."

She whipped up simple chicken salad sandwiches and put a cold bottle of milk on the middle of the table.

"Do you think you'll ever get married again, Faye?" I said between bites.

"I don't know. It's complicated."

"Just because you're divorced? Surely there must be some nice guys in the same boat who wouldn't judge you for that."

"It's a man's world, Adeline. The rules for them are different."

We finished up, and I helped clean the kitchen until it sparkled and then I found I couldn't stop myself from yawning.

"Your cot is where you left it on the porch. Try to get some sleep. Tomorrow is a new day."

The next morning I worked for Faye like no time had gone by since the day I ran off on Howard, when in fact a whole week had passed. Even though I came and went in the present at the exact moment, it didn't work like that when I left the past. Time went by at the regular speed here. They noticed that I'd left.

I spent the whole day glancing out the window, hoping that Howard would drop in.

I got my wish at the end of the day, while Faye and I were eating supper. The rumble of his truck pulled in along the side of the house and my stomach folded up into a little square as I mentally prepared to lay eyes on Howard again.

"Faye, I'm starving. Any grub?" he said as he breezed through the door like he owned the place. His blue eyes were as bright as ever, and a big happy grin stretched across his face.

Until he saw me. Then his lips inverted into a frown.

"Oh. I see you're babysitting. I'll come back later."

Ouch. That was a dig meant to hurt and it did. But I didn't want him to go. "No wait," I called. "We have lots."

I guess hunger trumped his damaged pride. He casually pulled out a chair next to Faye, away from me.

He ate the pork chops in record time, forcing small talk with Faye that excluded me, and then made a hasty exit.

"Wow," I said. "He's really ticked off at me."

"Howard doesn't take being stood up lightly. That's usually his job. Ya hurt his ego."

Babysitting, he'd said. He thought I was a child. I knew right then, what I had to do.

We did the dishes by hand afterward. I washed while Faye dried. "I need a favor," I said as I placed a soapy dish in the sink.

Faye rinsed it and picked it up. "What is it?"

"Remember the first day I came, and you thought I was a drop-in customer, but I couldn't decide what I wanted?"

She nodded.

"I do now. Will you cut my hair for me?"

"Right now?"

"Please?"

"I guess so. I'm booked up tomorrow, so I wouldn't be able to do it then anyway."

We finished the dishes and then she turned the lights on in the salon and I followed her inside. She motioned to one of the chairs. "Get in."

I grabbed a magazine before sitting down.

"What do you want?" Faye said, pumping the chair higher.

I opened the magazine and pointed to a picture of Marilyn Monroe. "That."

"That? Same color, too?"

"Yes." I was naturally blond from a long line of Scandinavians on my mother's side. Still, next to Marilyn, I didn't feel blond enough. "I want to go lighter and shorter." It was time to lose the ponytail.

"So, ya want to look like Marilyn Monroe, huh?" Faye draped the black salon cape over my torso and fastened it around my neck. "She's just another one of those fads, y'know? In a few years no one will even remember her name."

TEN

I COULDN'T STOP staring at myself in the bathroom mirror. I looked like Marilyn Monroe! Or maybe a Marilyn Monroe, slash, Scarlett Johansson blend, especially when I put on Faye's *Candy Apple Red* lipstick.

What would Howard think when he saw me now? I definitely looked older. Way older. And pretty hot, if I did say so myself.

The next day I spent all my time sweeping hair, cleaning counters and glancing out the window looking for Howard.

I really must have scared him off because it was three whole days before he stopped in again—I'd finished *Fahrenheit 451* and *The Martian Chronicles* and had started in on *The Illustrated Man* (Faye was a serious Bradbury fan). I'd almost given up on him.

He drove in at 4:37. I quickly checked my hair, applied *Tangerine Orange* lipstick and smoothed out my skirt. With the money Faye paid me, I'd bought a pair of black and white penny loafers and a cute little soft blue angora sweater at the ladies clothing store two blocks over.

When Howard strolled in he had the very reaction I'd dreamed he'd have.

"Whoa," he said, stopping in his tracks abruptly. "Who's the doll, Faye? What happened to the twig you had working before?"

Okay, not exactly like I dreamed. Did he really think I was a new worker? Or was he just being a *rotter*?

"Howard, stop being such a flirt," Faye said.

Howard circled around me like I was a show horse. "Adeline? Is that really you?" He whistled the sexy whistle.

Now that was what I'd been dreaming.

"You like it?" I said, using my sultry voice. (I didn't know I had a sultry voice.)

"You're a doll, I say! Hey, I was just going for a bite to eat, would you like to come along?"

Faye said, "You mean you didn't drop in here to raid my refrigerator?"

"Aw, c'mon." He worked his puppy-dog eyes on Faye. "Let me take the pretty girl out."

Faye turned to me. "Will you excuse us for a minute?" She grabbed her brother by the arm and practically dragged him out the front door. It was cracked open so I could hear her when she spoke. "You be careful with her, Howard. She's suffered enough heartache."

"I'm not doing anything she don't want to do."

Faye's voice lowered and I couldn't hear what else she said. After a couple minutes she came back in. Alone.

"Where's Howard?" I said. Did Faye really send him off?

"He's waiting for you in his truck. Look, Adeline, I know

I'm not your mother, but as a guest in my home, I'm asking that ya come home by ten o'clock."

Faye was giving me a curfew. Boundaries. Like a mother. Instead of making me angry it made me happy. Really happy. I ran to her and gave her a big angora sweater on angora sweater hug.

I slowed down when I reached the corner of the shop, not wanting to look like a skipping school girl. If Howard was channeling his inner James Dean, I would channel my inner Marilyn Monroe.

When Howard saw me, he rushed to the passenger door and opened it. The way he stared at me as I got in gave me goose bumps. No one had ever looked at me like that. It made me feel sexy and very grown up.

Howard kept sneaking glances at me as we drove through Hollywood's back streets and turned onto Sunset Boulevard. I felt my cheeks warm with his obvious admiration.

He parked on the street when we reached our destination and rushed over to open my door for me. I *loved* being treated like a lady. It was perfectly fine to wear dainty, white gloves in the fifties which I did, and was glad of it when he took my hand.

I gasped a little when I saw where we were eating. Schwab's Pharmacy! I was new to Hollywood but I did know a bit about the fame of this place and had seen glimpses of it in movies like *Sunset Boulevard* and *The Majestic*.

You don't normally expect much from a pharmacy, but Schwab's was also a diner and a place that stars, and agents looking for the next star liked to hang out in the fifties.

It was long and narrow on the inside with the diner portion running down the full length of the right hand wall. A chest-high glass display case ran down the middle, showcasing colognes and perfumes. On the left wall you could find all kinds of sundry items, from magazines like TIME and HARPER, to candies to band-aids. It may not have sounded like much, but it was busy, full of men in suits wearing fedoras, and women in thick stockings and funny hats.

It no longer existed in my time, having been bulldozed and turned into a boring retail complex.

I tried to keep the look of amazement off my face.

"Hey, Howard!" Three guys and a girl sat in the leather-back stools along the diner and waved us over.

"Who's the new dame?" one of the guys said loud enough to be heard over the din.

"This here is Adeline," Howard said while draping his arm around my shoulders. Here it was. It was happening! Howard was practically hugging me and it was just as I imagined—thrilling.

"She's new to town," Howard continued. "Adeline, this is Benny."

The loud talker swiveled and shook my hand. His eyes appraised me with approval.

"And Leroy, Judy and Elmer." Judy was a pretty girl with red hair done much the same as mine, and voluptuous curves. She wore a cotton white shirt and a tangerine flared skirt with matching tangerine neck scarf and lipstick. She had her legs crossed and she swung her foot, wearing the iconic black and white patent leather shoes. She smiled warmly at me as I sat down next to her, and I felt hopeful that I had another friend.

Elmer sat on her opposite side and had an arm possessively around her shoulders.

"So, where ya from?" Benny asked.

"Across town," I said, remaining vague.

Howard jumped in. "She works for my sister."

"Adeline," Judy said. "Such a pretty name."

"Thanks."

"Are y'new here? I don't remember you from school."

"Uh, yeah, I'm new. I don't go to school. Here."

"Well, ya gotta job." She winked at Howard. "And a man, what else does a girl need?"

She laughed and I felt myself blush.

"Oh, honey." She reached over to tap my arm. "You and I will be best friends, I can tell."

A waitress approached our section of the counter, all smiles and flirty eyes. She was a pretty girl, even in her cotton smock and apron. Howard's friends gave her the same attention as they had me, and it irked me a little. I watched Howard's reaction to the attractive waitress, but he all but ignored her, ordering us both hamburgers and sodas. He turned his attention directly back to me.

Swoon.

Judy sipped root beer through a straw, her eyes darting toward Leroy every few minutes. My instinct told me that Judy would rather have Leroy's arm around her shoulders than Elmer's.

I couldn't blame her. Leroy had dark hair, slicked back in the typical "duck bill" fashion of the times, wore a black leather jacket and had dark eyes that brooded. There was something dangerous and off limits about him.

And he kept stealing glances at me. It made me nervous, but kind of excited, that a guy like him would find a girl like me glance worthy.

Howard noticed, too, I thought. He tightened his hold on my shoulder.

When Judy's eyes weren't settling on Leroy, they were scouring the room.

"Are you expecting someone?" I asked, sipping my soda.

Judy patted her hair. "No one in particular. But they say Lana Turner was discovered here by an agent just come in for coffee. Ya never know who you'll meet here."

"You're looking for an agent?"

"Aren't we all?"

Uh, no.

"I'd love to be in pictures. It's so glamorous," Judy practically purred. Then she whispered in my ear, "And they make so much money."

She leaned back again, giggling, and pulled a metal case, the size of a slim paperback, out of her purse. She clicked it open and drew out a cigarette. She extended her arm to me. "You want one?"

I shook my head. "Don't smoke."

"Really?"

She got in two quick puffs before our burgers came, and then she tapped her cigarette out in the communal ashtray.

When we were finished eating, we said goodbye to Howard's friends.

"So long, Adeline," Judy said, and I waved.

We walked arm in arm back to Howard's truck, where he opened the passenger door for me and helped me in. A girl could get used to this.

He held my gloved hand as we drove, except for when he had to shift gears, all the way back to Faye's house. *That's All Right* by Elvis Presley played on the radio.

"See, Adeline?" Howard's eyes lit up. "This is the music of the future. "Rock and Roll. Faye doesn't get it. Doesn't like that I want to play this kind of music, but Rock and Roll is around to stay. It's making lots of people a truck load of money and I'm going to get my share."

I smiled back, knowing that he was right about the future of Rock, but a little worm nagged the back of my mind. If Howard succeeded as a musician, why hadn't I heard of him?

We arrived at Faye's and I pushed that thought out of my mind.

Howard didn't get out of the truck. Instead he reached for my hand. My heart played its own Rock and Roll show.

"You're so pretty, Adeline."

Drum solo.

"I'm afraid if I don't swoop y'up, some other lucky fellow's gonna beat me to it."

What was he saying? Then I thought of Leroy and wondered if Howard was thinking of him, too.

"Will ya be my girl?"

My heart was breaking guitars on the stage now. Was I having an attack right in front of Howard? *Move lips, move.*

They didn't, so I just nodded. Okay.

Then, he leaned in. Oh, my goodness, he was going to kiss me! But wait—I can't. I *can't* kiss him because it might trigger it. I might travel and disappear right in front of Howard.

Why didn't I think of this before? I had no idea this situation would be thrust upon me so quickly. I pulled away slightly.

"Too fast, huh?" he said, stopping midway. "That's okay. I can wait."

Just then the light over the door flicked on and off several times. "What's that?" I whispered.

"Faye. She's afraid I'm going to push ya into something y'don't want to do. She thinks she's your mother."

"Why didn't Faye have kids?" I was thankful for the change of subject and that he was okay that I didn't kiss him tonight. "I mean, when she was married."

"Faye can't have kids. They tried, her and Jack, but after five years, the doctors gave up on them, and then Jack gave up on her. He wanted kids, so he went off in search of a new wife who could produce what Faye couldn't."

"That sucks," I said.

He looked at me and smiled. "You say funny things sometimes, Adeline."

Oh, no. Did I just make myself look stupid?

"But, I like that about ya. You're sweet."

"I should go," I said, picturing Faye at the light switch. He nodded, jumped out and opened my door. When we got to the house, I thought I should warn him, somehow.

"Howard, I live on the other side of town. Sometimes I have to leave, when my father is home. Sometimes, quite suddenly."

"That's okay."

I wondered if he would insist on driving me there (when I had to go) and on meeting my dad, but he didn't. Of course, that was a good thing. But, it bothered me a little.

"Well, good night," I said, turning the doorknob.

"Good night, Adeline," he said. Then, before I could protest, he pecked me lightly on the forehead. I breathed in sharply. Nothing. No dizziness, no light.

Just giddy happiness.

ELEVEN

HOWARD DROPPED BY Faye's salon in the morning. "Hey, Faye, can I borrow Adeline for a few minutes?"

Faye shrugged. I had a feeling she had a hard time saying no to him and he knew it. I followed him out to his truck.

"It's so good to see you," he said. Then he leaned in and kissed me.

Hello? *Call me surprised.* I held my breath at first, waiting for the dizziness to start, but when it didn't, I let myself kiss him back. That was the advantage of living in the past—as far as kissing went, anyway—I had warning. If I felt dizzy, I could leave Howard in time before he saw me disappear, though it might be hard to explain to him where I went all of a sudden, and why I didn't come back.

If I took that chance in my present, there was no warning. My kissing partner would travel with me, and that would be a bad scene. Another reason why having a boyfriend in the past would just work out better for me.

So, I spent a couple minutes kissing Howard, and it was

wonderful. He'd obviously had some practice at this, and I hoped I wasn't coming off as a beginner. Was I doing it right?

Then he pulled away and sighed. "I have to go away for a while."

What? "Why?" Just my luck. When things started to go great, wham, bad news curve ball.

"Work. I'm going north to pick grapes. Elmer is going, too. It's too far to drive back and forth so we're staying at the pickers' cabins at the vineyard."

"But what about your work here, your music?"

"That gig is over, and I ain't got nothing lined up. I need the dough."

I was overwhelmed with disappointment. I had no idea how long I would be here, and if I'd even be here when he got back.

I felt Howard's finger under my chin, pulling my face back up to his.

"I'm sorry to leave ya, baby. I won't be gone too long, just one or two weeks, tops."

I forced a smile, for his sake. He was being so sweet.

One last kiss, soft and delicious, and then I watched him drive away.

I pulled myself together before going back into the salon. Faye's customer was under the hair dryer. Faye took a good look at my eyes—I couldn't help that I was tearing up—and pulled me to the back of the room, "What'd he do to ya?"

"Nothing. I mean he didn't do anything to me. He's going up north to pick grapes at a vineyard."

"Oh, right. He'd mentioned that."

"He says he'll be gone a week or two."

All Faye had to say about that was, "Well, at least I'll save money on groceries for a while."

I was hoping for a little more sympathy, but I guess that was all I was going to get from Faye.

Later that night, Faye opened the small freezer that was inside her fridge. You had to open the single fridge door first to open the smaller one at the top inside. "Look what I finally bought," she said, pulling out a flat rectangular package. "TV dinners. Have ya seen these before, Adeline? They're new. A whole meal—meat, potatoes and vegetables—in one tin-foil pan. Ya just throw it into the oven. Hardly no work or mess at all. Just like the commercials say, great for working women like me."

I nodded. "Yeah, I've seen those before."

"Oh, probably with living with just your dad, huh? Men can't cook worth beans, I know."

Well, some men can, but not my dad.

Faye ripped off the paper covering and tossed it into her oven. "I didn't get a chance to tell ya earlier, but I'm going out tonight. Will you be okay alone?"

Faye was going out?

"I stay home alone all the time. I'll be fine," I said. "So, what's going on tonight?"

"Actually, I have a date."

A date? Faye? That was why she only put in one TV dinner. Not because it was big enough to share, but for me to eat by myself.

"Really? Wow, I didn't know you had a boyfriend? That's great." I said this, but I didn't feel it at all. In fact, I felt annoyed. Why didn't I want Faye to date? I was being silly. And selfish.

"I don't know if I'd call him my boyfriend, though we have gone out a few times. I don't think he's seeing anyone else, and I'm not seeing anyone else, so I guess you could call him my boyfriend."

She's seen him before? Why didn't I know this?

Faye went to her room but left the door ajar. I could see her change from her workday clothes to her evening wear. I had a flashback of my mother, also getting ready to go out somewhere with my dad. The image was faint, like an old black and white photograph. Somehow my memory had lost its color.

"So, what's his name?" I said a little too loudly. "What's he like?"

Faye came out of her bedroom looking very sharp in a slim-fitting, cotton dress with a wide belt and heels. "His name is Larry." She went to the bathroom and started putting on makeup. "And he's nice."

"Where'd you meet him?"

Faye took a deep breath. "He and his wife were friends of mine and my ex-husband. His wife passed away last year. We met up at the bank a few weeks ago and started chatting. That evening he telephoned me and asked me to dinner." She paused to apply lipstick; I recognized it as *Milk Chocolate*. "I was tired of eating alone, so I thought why not? It turned out to be a very pleasant evening."

A very pleasant evening? Did that mean he kissed her on the first date?

There was a knock on the door. Faye turned to me. "Can you get that?" She disappeared back into her bedroom.

I opened the side door, the main entrance to the house portion of the building, and there stood a tall man wearing a tan color suit, white shirt and narrow, black tie. His hair, graying at the temples was greased back like every other man's in this era. He had a fedora hat in his hands. And, I had to admit, he wasn't bad looking for an older guy.

"Good evening," he said. "I'm Larry and you must be Adeline."

Faye told him about me? "Yes, I am. Please, come in. Faye will be ready in a couple minutes."

I wondered if I was supposed to offer him a drink or take his hat or ask him to sit? I didn't know how to play hostess in the fifties. Thankfully, I was spared having to make a choice about it because Faye came out. She had a hat on. It was form fitting like a swimmers cap that had netting and flowers attached. It made her look really dignified and pretty.

Hrumph. Usually it was Faye watching me get ready to go out. I never thought about what it was like for her when I left. I didn't like the feeling, and I didn't want her to go out with this Larry, even though I was sure he was a nice guy.

Was this how she felt about me going out with her brother? I'd have to be more sensitive to her in the future.

"Adeline, the meal in the oven should be ready for you in about five minutes. Larry and I shouldn't be late, but don't feel like you have to wait up for me."

Was that a hint? Was she not planning on coming home tonight? I felt panic at the thought. First of all, yeah, I didn't relish spending the night alone here, and second, I didn't want her with Larry. I knew I was being irrational and selfish but I couldn't help myself.

I forced a stiff smile. "I'll be fine. Have fun."

Larry opened the door for Faye and led her out by the arm. I could hear her laughing through the closed door.

I just stood there. Here I was alone in Faye's house. It was too quiet. In a daze, I walked to the boxy TV and turned it on. Manually, since of course they didn't have remotes. A variety show of some kind was on; a man was spinning plates on long sticks. The picture and sound were fuzzy. I turned the volume down, not really caring to watch it. I just wanted the company.

The buzzer on the oven went off, and I hurried to the kitchen because the buzz noise was really annoying. And, I realized, I was hungry and I didn't want it to burn. I turned off the buzzer, and took out my supper with oven mitts. I pulled back the tin foil and wrinkled my nose.

Not at all like homemade, the liars.

I picked at my meal, watching a scratchy black and white version of *I Love Lucy* on the TV.

I threw the TV dinner tray in the trash when I finished and tidied up the kitchen. I returned to the living room and scouted Faye's book shelf. There was a row of sci-fi novels I hadn't heard of and a selection of sci-fi short fiction magazines called *Fantastic Adventures, Planet Stories* and *Wonder Stories.*

Faye sure liked her science fiction stories.

On a small shelf to the right sat two black and white photos propped up in plastic frames. I had noticed them earlier but hadn't taken a good look at them before now.

The first one was of a middle aged couple standing in front of a very old car, maybe from the nineteen-thirties. I guessed they were Faye and Howard's parents.

The second photo was of a girl in her early teens, sitting with a baby on her lap. The girl was obviously Faye, same bright eyes and wide smile, and same contagious happy countenance. The baby must be Howard. I didn't realize how much older Faye was than Howard, since she looked and acted younger.

Maybe, she wouldn't be too young for my dad, after all. Hmm.

I heard an engine pull into the drive and my first impulse was that Howard came home early. I sprang to the door, opening it wide.

Only it wasn't Howard. It was Leroy.

He smirked when he saw me. "Well, hello, doll," he said with a raspy voice.

"Hi?"

He leaned up against the house and lit a cigarette. The collar of his leather jacket stood to attention much like my nerves. Leroy oozed danger, and I took a small step back.

"What do you want?"

"Well, I want something Howard owes me."

"Howard's not here."

"Maybe his sister can cover it."

"She's not here either."

Leroy let out a long stream of smoke through pursed lips as his dark eyes scanned my body. I took a full step back inside the house, inwardly cursing myself for giving it away that I was home alone.

"I see. Well, you tell ol' Howard if I don't get my money soon, I'll just take payment in another form."

Leroy took one last puff of his smoke before dropping it and grinding it under his foot. He sauntered to his car, a new looking Ford convertible, and saluted me before backing out.

I closed the door and locked it tight.

Then I went to the back porch to lock it, too, grabbing my

book from the cot before doing so. There was no way I'd sleep out there tonight, just easy pickings for Leroy.

My insides hadn't stopped turning and I curled up on the sofa, hugging one of Faye's cushions.

What kind of trouble had Howard gotten himself into?

I had no intention of falling asleep before Faye got home. Once my heart settled, I flipped open *The Illustrated Man*, needing the distraction. It was a series of short stories, all with an out-of-this-world twist. I read story after story, checking the clock after each one. Finally at 1:30 am, I heard the click of the lock on the door. Faye was giggling and whispering.

I sat up.

"Adeline?" Her eyes narrowed as she took me in. "You're still awake?" Not only had I surprised them, I think Faye was a little ticked off, but I didn't care.

"I just got so into this book," I said faking a yawn. "I lost track of time. It's a really, really good book."

I didn't know if they'd had other plans, but Larry, a true gentleman, kindly excused himself and said good night, capably diffusing what could have been an awkward situation.

I could see why Faye liked him.

Faye sat down and removed her gloves and then her shoes. "You read that whole book tonight?"

"Yeah, I'm a fast reader. So, did you have a good time?" I said. Also, meaning, did it take you until 1:30 am to eat your dinner?

"Yes, very nice."

Her eyes went all glossy when she said that. I knew it wasn't any of my business but I couldn't help but ask, "Do you think you and Larry will get married?"

She sat up a bit when I said that. "Um, I don't know. It's a little early in the relationship to think about that."

"But if he asked you," I persisted, "would you?"

"Maybe. I don't really like the idea of growing old alone."

"That's not a good reason to get married though, is it?" A black snake wrapped around my chest, and I found it hard to breathe. For some reason the thought of Faye marrying Larry terrified me. "Shouldn't you be in love first?"

"That would be ideal. Love can look a lot of different ways. For instance it would probably look differently for me, at my stage of life than it would for you."

She thought I was talking about Howard. At another time, maybe, but right now I was just thinking about what would happen to me if Faye and Larry got married. They wouldn't want a random teen hanging around while they were newly-weds, if ever.

The black snake squeezed harder. I should have known better. I should have taken a lot of deep, calming breaths.

Because I felt dizzy. I was going back to the twenty-first century and Faye was sitting right across from me in the living room. She was about to watch me vanish right before her eyes.

I made a decision. I stepped across the room in two strides and grabbed Faye's bare arm.

Good thing she liked science fiction.

TWELVE

I'D NEVER IN A ZILLION years forget the look on Faye's face as we tumbled through the light, her mouth open, releasing a thin scream. I still had her arm when the falling sensation along with the brightness passed.

"It's okay, Faye. You're all right."

Her eyes were wide, glassy with fright. And as she stared at me I realized with regret that I was the object of her fear. She was afraid of *me*.

"You're fine, I promise. I'll explain everything." I felt like I had to reassure her. "You're safe. No one will hurt you."

My dad threw open the front door and then stopped short in his tracks. That was right. When I'd "left" he had been chasing me because I'd just caught him kissing the blonde.

"Adeline?" His gazed flitted back and forth from me to Faye. I was wearing the same clothes as before, fifties style shorts and baggy T-shirt. Faye wore her glamorous fifties evening wear. She still had the hat on, but stood on our front tile patio in nylon feet. Of course, she had just taken off her shoes.

"What happened to your hair?" Dad finally sputtered. Oh yeah. My ponytail that I'd had since I was five was gone.

"Um, Dad, this is my friend, Faye. Faye, this is my dad."

Dad tentatively extended his hand. Faye's hand trembled as she reached out to shake it.

"Dad, I think Faye could use a drink." I led Faye into our house, and Dad followed behind us. Faye's mouth gaped open. I tried to see everything from her perspective. Big, puffy leather sectional in the living room across from a gas fireplace with a huge flat screen TV hanging above it. Half naked girls were traipsing down a runway—probably America's Top Model—in color and high definition.

The kitchen had all the top of the line stainless steel appliances, including a massive two-door refrigerator, a monster compared to what Faye had, and a dishwasher and microwave. The cabinets reached the ceiling and a tabletop sized island stood in the middle. All the countertops were white speckled granite.

Our kitchen was bigger than her whole house.

I gestured for her to take a seat at our table, which happened to be made out of thick slabs of oak. No chrome or Formica here.

My dad brought Faye a glass of water.

"Dad, I think she needs something stronger than that," I said. Dad saw Faye's shaken state and agreed. He poured her a glass of wine, emptying the bottle he'd been sharing with the blonde.

She was still curled up on the sofa, but had a scowl on her face. I imagined she didn't like the idea of competition. I gave her a sour look that suggested maybe she should leave. She took the hint; I'd have to give her credit for that.

"David, I think I'll be going," she said, getting up. If she was hoping for a protest from Dad, she didn't' get it. That made me very happy. Dad did walk her to the door, though, to see her off. I couldn't think about what they were doing and I just hoped he wasn't kissing her good night.

Faye gulped down her wine, and then turned to me. "What's going on Adeline? What just happened?"

I pulled out another chair and sat down. "You're a fan of science fiction so I'm hoping you will believe what I'm about to tell you." I breathed in deeply. I'd never told another soul my secret before. "I'm a time traveler."

Faye studied my face, her eyelids blinking in high speed. "A time traveler?"

"Yes. I only travel to 1955, kind of a loop. Well, time goes by for me back there, too, so it's 1955 now. I leave my time in my present and loop to your time, your present. Back and forth. I don't know why, and I can't control it. It just happens."

Faye's hand went to her throat. "What year is it, here?"

"Two-thousand-twelve."

A soft "oh" left her lips. Faye's eyes turned back into her head and she flopped over. Dad had entered just at that moment and helped me catch her.

"What's wrong with her?" he said.

"She fainted." We carried her to the sofa and laid her down gently. I removed her hat, which was secured with Bobby pins, and covered her legs with a flannel blanket.

I sat on the sectional by her feet. Dad sat on the other piece, facing me.

"Your eyes are black like you've been double punched,

your hair is suddenly shorter, you have a friend, not your age, who's dressed very convincingly in retro," Dad said. "She's here without shoes and now has fainted on our sofa. What's going on, Adeline?"

I looked at Faye, still unconscious, and wondered—did I just make a huge mistake? Should we call an ambulance? Would she even have a valid Social Security Number? Even if she did, no one would believe she was almost ninety years old.

I'd just told Faye my secret. The only person ever. Well, except for that one girl back in Cambridge, who claimed to be a time traveler, too. I didn't even remember her name. How dense of me not to take the time to ask her more questions, see how she dealt with her "situation."

Now, in my new quest for friends, I wished I had made that girl one.

I stared back at my dad. He deserved answers, didn't he? Should I tell him? Would he believe me?

"Dad," I heard myself say, "she's from the year 1955. I'm a time traveler."

A wave of disappointment crossed his face. "Adeline, I'm not in the mood for jokes."

Great, he didn't believe me. "I'm not joking. The first time it happened I was ten, just after mom died."

Dad stood up. I could tell he was frustrated with me. "I'm going to clean the kitchen. Let me know when she awakens."

I moved to the floor, and knelt by Faye's face. "Faye? Faye? Wake up." I tapped her cheek and she groaned softly.

"Faye? Are you all right?"

Faye opened her eyes, looked at me and then the space she was in. She closed her eyes and groaned again. "I was hoping this was just a dream," she muttered.

"We have a guest room, Faye. How about I take you to it? You can have a good sleep, and then we can work on getting you home tomorrow." I had no idea how I was going to keep that promise, but Faye mouthed "Okay," and let me help her up.

The guest room had its own bathroom. Luxury, really, compared to Faye's place.

I left her sitting on the bed as I ran for an extra set of my pajamas. I sprinted back down the hall and dashed into her room. I could see that some color had returned to her face. That was a relief.

"Adeline?"

"Yeah?"

"I'm very tired. And confused. And a little angry. Just so y'know."

"I get that. Let's work it out over breakfast, tomorrow, okay?"

I left her alone and for the millionth time wondered what in the world I was thinking?

When I went back to the kitchen, Dad was leaning against the cleaned off island, his hand on his chin.

"I've seen a lot of strange things since moving to Hollywood, Adeline, and I'm sure you have, too, but I never thought we'd become one of those strange things."

"I know. Look, I'm exhausted. Let's talk about it tomorrow, okay?"

He nodded and I trudged off to my own bed, which, I had to admit, was bliss.

. . .

THE NEXT MORNING I woke up early, my memories of the events of the night before not leaving me, even in my dreams. I jumped out of bed to find Faye.

To my surprise she was sitting at the kitchen table, fully dressed in her glamour clothes, eating breakfast with my dad!

"Good morning, Adeline," Dad said. Faye added her greeting. I could see that Dad had gone all out. Faye seemed happy, too. I *knew* it. I knew they would have chemistry together.

Dad motioned to an empty chair, a spot at the table with a place setting ready for me.

I joined them, curious as to what they might have been talking about. "Did you sleep well, Faye?"

"Yes, I did, thanks. Your father has been a great host to me already today." Faye took a sip of coffee, espresso with foamed milk, actually, from Dad's high tech cappuccino maker. There was nothing like it from where she came from, I knew.

"You have a very lovely home, Adeline. I can't imagine what y'must think of my place. Is it still standing, I wonder?"

No, it wasn't, but I didn't think I needed to get into that yet. "So, you're okay, with all, um, this?"

"I don't really have a choice, do I?"

Not at the moment. My father cleared his throat, keeping me from having to answer. "Adeline, I'm trying to understand."

It felt really good when I'd finally told him last night, even though he didn't believe me. It was worth another shot.

"It seems that I have this *gift*, if you can call it that. Sometimes, I go back in time. I travel on this loop to the fifties."

My dad just offered a blank look. Confusion, but I thought I could see a desire in his eyes to believe me.

I continued, "That's where I met Faye. She's been really great to me, Dad, helping me when I was alone."

"I see." He smiled at Faye, but I could tell it was forced. "Well, I guess I should be thankful for that. But when exactly have you been gone to the past? I haven't noticed you missing." He was still not fully believing.

"That's because no time goes by on this end. I come and go at the exact same moment. The only difference is when I return to here, my present, I have dark rings under my eyes."

"Like last night?"

"Yes. And that's why to you, I walked outside with a pony-tail, and by the time you got to me, my hair was cut. Faye did it by the way. Isn't it great?"

Dad paused before answering. I think he was trying to put the pieces together. "Your hair does look nice," he finally said. He glanced at Faye, "You do look the part." Then back to me. "When did this—" He waved his hand around not able, it seemed, to say the words "—time travel all start?"

"When I was ten." Like I'd already told him last night.

"Ten? Back in Cambridge." He went *hmm*. "Just after your mother died."

I nodded. For the first time since we arrived in California Dad's face went into that flat contrite look, like canvas stretched across a frame. "Dad? Are you okay?"

Faye sat her empty coffee cup on the table. "I'm authentic, if that's what you're thinking."

But that wasn't what he was thinking. I knew that for sure. He was thinking about Mom.

Faye went on. "And as shocked as y'must be, Mr. Savoy, I'm even more shocked. I'm the one who came to your time, and not you to mine. I can't deny that I'm here and that Adeline brought me."

She was trying to help me and I was grateful. I wanted my

dad to make sense of what I was saying so he wouldn't think I was a freak or worse, crazy.

An awkward silence ascended and I saw Dad checking his watch. What should we do now? It could be a long day, just waiting around for something to trigger a trip back to 1955. Faye looked perkier this morning. Maybe she was up for a little futuristic sci-fi adventure after all.

"Dad, why don't we take Faye on a tour? Faye, wouldn't you like to see the sights?"

"Are there flying saucers and little green men?"

I grinned. "Uh, no. But, I'm sure you will spot people equally as strange."

THIRTEEN

"I'LL GET MY KEYS."

I still couldn't tell if Dad was buying the time travel story, but he was playing along well if he didn't.

"I don't have any shoes," Faye said, pointing her toes.

"That's all right," I said. "I have a pair of flip-flops you can borrow."

"Flip-flops?"

"Sandals. And I'll lend you a summer dress." I was excited to show Faye around. Maybe she would really like it here and not want to go back. Maybe she would really like my dad and want to live with us. I smiled at the thought. That would be so cool.

I brought her the dress and flip-flops. Her eyebrows arched as she accepted them. She remained silent as she closed the door to her room.

I heard the garage door open while Faye changed. Dad backed the Mustang out into the driveway and waited. The top was already down.

"You look nice," I said when Faye walked out. She lacked the sophisticated flare that hats and nylons brought on, but casual worked for her, too. Even if she didn't think so.

"It's okay to go out in public like this? Bare legs and feet?"

"Yes, it's more than okay." I was dressed similarly. I grabbed her arm. "Let's go."

She didn't get far before stopping in her tracks and her jaw slacking. She stared at our new model Mustang—sleek and shiny—and nothing like the classic 1950s cousin.

"That's a beautiful car," she finally mustered.

"Thanks," Dad said, looking suave and macho in sunglasses.

I opened the front door for Faye and got into the back seat behind Dad. Dad headed for Hollywood Boulevard and I watched Faye's profile. Her expression vacillated between awe and fear, which, I supposed, were kind of the same thing.

The biggest change from her time was open space—or the lack of it. Where there was once open fields and green space, now it was nothing but strip malls, subdivisions and people.

Dad found a place to park and I helped Faye out of the car. She still seemed a little shaky to me and I wondered belatedly if maybe we were rushing things. I hooked my arm through hers and she didn't let go.

I tried to see things through Faye's eyes. More traffic with hardly a 1950s vehicle to be seen, more shops with not one recognizable name, and most of all more people–of every size, shape and color.

The buildings were taller and so were the advertisements. Closed-up shops were covered in graffiti. Enormous billboards displayed beautiful near naked models in underwear ads, and promos for the latest movie release. Everything was much louder, bolder and more liberal.

She pressed into me with a nervous shudder as we navigated the crowds, a mix of-locals and tourists.

"Is this really the same boulevard?"

I nodded.

We walked by street performers, dressed in the latest movie character costumes and others doing circus tricks—walking on stilts, juggling—all hoping for a dollar or two to be dropped in their hat or box. I felt Faye flinch as we squeezed by.

"Everything is so—different. I hardly recognize it," she said in a soft voice, like a frightened child.

"There's Grauman's Chinese Theater," I pointed out. "It's still here." Though it had changed, too. "And..." I motioned toward the historic twelve-storey, Spanish-style building across the street. "The Roosevelt Hotel."

We paused in front of the theater, jostling with the tourists who were taking pictures with what must have looked like miniature cameras to Faye.

"I see they finally tore down the Hollywood Hotel."

I recalled passing by the old relic while driving with Howard. The Kodak Theater had been built in its place along with a huge mall. People swarmed in and out.

Faye's eyes scanned the crowds. "Where are all the white people?"

I knew Faye wasn't being racist, just observant. Hollywood, like most of California, had seen an explosion in ethnic cultures. Every other restaurant was either Indian, Korean or Thai. Plus, Spanish could be heard everywhere you went. Very different from her time.

"Oh, we're still here, Faye, but it's cool to be able to share space with people of every culture, don't you think?"

"Oh, ya, of course." Her eyes settled on a row of teens waiting at a bus stop. "What do all the kids have in their ears?"

"Those are called iPods. The white cords lead to little speakers in their ears. It's how you listen to the music."

"Like a radio? I can't see anything."

"That's because with technology things get really small. The iPods are small enough to fit in their pockets."

She nodded like she understood, but I didn't think she did. Then she pointed to the sidewalk.

"What are these stars?"

"Oh, this is the Walk of Fame. It commemorates people who have succeeded in show business in some way."

"Olivia Newton John, Jack Nicholson, Godzilla?" Faye shook her head. "I don't recognize these names."

Dad was gawking at the sidewalk, too. "And over here is Walter Disney," he said.

"Oh, I heard of him," Faye said. "He just opened up a theme park in Anaheim."

"Well, it turned out to be very successful," I told her. "There's another one in Florida now."

"Really?"

We crossed the street and kept walking east.

"Here are some you'll know." I pointed to other stars imbedded in the cement while people scooted around us. "The Spinners. Marilyn Monroe."

"So, she made something of herself, after all."

I smiled. "You could say that."

We stopped at the Farmers Market near Vine. Dad bought fresh mushrooms and peppers along with a fillet of Salmon.

"For lunch," he said.

On the way back to the car we passed by a group of boys, whose pants hung half way down their rear ends. They wore excessive bling around their necks and hooped earrings in their ears. Some of them had shaved heads, and even though we were walking with Dad, they eyeballed Faye and me in a gross way. One of them was blasting rap music into the street. I recognized the cuter one as Candace's boyfriend, Dan Highland. I quickly averted my eyes.

"Is that how the kids turn out these days?" Faye said.

"Not all of them," I said, feeling apologetic.

Faye craned her neck back to stare. "And what is that awful noise?"

"Kanye West."

Faye stopped abruptly and pinched the bridge of her nose. She squeezed her eyes shut, taking deep breaths.

"You really do find this upsetting, don't you?" my dad said. I didn't miss the sincere concern on his face and how he tenderly patted her on the back.

Out here, on the busy, modern streets of Hollywood, Faye looked small and fragile to me, like a glass doll. This brought out a protectiveness in Dad I'd hadn't seen since Mom had gotten sick.

It didn't sit well with me. I felt the monster nudge in my gut again. It wasn't that I didn't want Dad to care about Faye, but *I* wanted that kind of response from my father. *I* was his daughter after all. Didn't he know *I* needed him to comfort and protect *me*?

I knew I was being petty. "Maybe we should head back," I said, feeling deflated.

It was a quiet ride home. Though it was September the air

was warm. And dry, not damp with humidity like what I was used to in Cambridge. The tall palm trees waved like a receiving line. Not an autumn leaf turning red anywhere to be seen.

Marco was sitting on the curb when we got home. For some reason his presence in our threesome irked me. He wasn't a part of Faye's life. I huffed at the idea that he was about to intrude.

Of course, when he saw us, he sauntered over and I was forced to make introductions.

"Faye, this is my neighbor, Marco." I wondered if he caught that I didn't call him friend. I could be a real bag sometimes.

"Marco, this is my, our, friend Faye."

"Pleased to meet you," Marco said, always the gentleman. They shook hands.

Then, my dad went ahead and invited him for lunch. Oh, brother. How were we ever going to discuss what was really going on now, with Marco there?

Dad lit the barbecue on the patio and started grilling the salmon and vegetables he'd bought at the Farmers Market. I busied myself with setting the patio table, not even looking at Marco and trying hard to forgive him for infringing on my time with Dad and Faye (and my secret agenda to get them to fall for each other).

Faye watched Dad as he flipped the salmon. She asked him where the briquettes were and my dad explained how it cooked with gas. My heart did a happy dance when I saw them talking together. Dad even got Faye to smile a little.

"Faye's just visiting from, uh, out of town," I said to Marco who had taken a seat at the table. I couldn't ignore him forever.

He'd figure out that I was ticked off, and then start analyzing me, which would just tick me off even more.

It didn't take long for the salmon to be done. We sat on the back deck, shaded by the large patio umbrella. Once we were all dished out and had completed our polite requests to pass things around, the conversation started to lag, leaving that awful awkward dead space and the sound of our cutlery scraping the stoneware. Dad finally got up and put some music on. Faye had fallen into a daze—not at all like the strong, spunky person I knew. My heart's little happy dance faltered, and deep down I knew that Faye and Dad wouldn't work out.

"Hey, Adeline," Marco said when he'd swallowed his last bite. "Do you want to go do something?" Suddenly, I felt relieved to escape the deadness here.

"Go, ahead," Dad said. I wondered if he was hoping for some alone time with Faye, but then she excused herself, saying she was tired and needed to lie down.

What a big mess I had made!

"You look out of sorts," Marco said when we got outside. I stopped in my tracks and scowled at him.

"Okay." He put two hands in the air as in surrender. "I won't analyze; I promise. I'm just concerned as your friend."

"I'm fine." I managed a smile. "Sorry, for being so grumpy all the time."

"You are kind of grumpy." He grinned. "But I have just the thing to cheer you up."

I smelled it as soon as he opened the door to his house. Sweet, yummy, chocolateness.

"You made chocolate cookies?"

"Yeah. For you."

I felt my face free fall with an expression that said, *"We're just friends!"*

"For fun, Adeline," he added quickly. "Remember that? Fun?"

I forced my expression into a quick recovery. "Oh, I know."

Marco proceeded to get out two glasses and filled them with milk. He handed me my glass, and after picking up the plate of cookies, he led me to the living room. His little sister was playing *Mario*.

"Oh, Marco!" I practically swallowed the first cookie whole. "These are amazing!"

With a mouthful he muffled something back that resembled "I'm glad you like them."

We watched Mario race through colorful obstacles, until his little sister jumped up and shouted, "Hurray! I beat the level."

"That's great, Ally," Marco said, wiping cookie crumbs from his face. Let us have a turn."

"Oh," I said quickly. "I don't know how to play."

"You've never played Mario? What kind of childhood did you have?" Marco handed me a second controller.

"Actually, it kind of sucked."

"Well, it's never too late." Marco leaned in close to show me how to use the control. I could smell his sweet chocolate cookie breath, and when his hand brushed against mine, I tensed a little, surprised by how he made me feel. Aware. Nervous.

Then he settled back into the sofa, a safe, friendly distance away from me, and we started the game.

And he was right. It was fun.

. . .

"I HAVE AN AUDITION!" Dad said, his face wide with excitement. "I almost missed the email. So, sorry, but I have to rush out."

He turned to Faye. She'd roused from her nap and was enjoying one of Marco's cookies' I'd brought over.

"I'll see you when I get back."

She nodded. "Sure."

Dad left and Faye started pacing the kitchen floor. She pointed to the microwave. "What is that, anyway?"

"Well, it's a microwave. It uses, well, microwaves to heat up food. Basically, it stirs the atoms in the food up extremely fast creating heat. It cooks food really fast."

"Oh."

I couldn't tell if she understood or not.

"What about that?" She pointed to Dad's laptop he'd left on the table.

"That's a computer."

"A computer?" Her face widened in amazement, a look I was getting used to seeing on her face. "In your house? That you can carry around?"

"I know, like I said before, with technology, everything gets smaller."

Faye's shoulders slumped. She closed her eyes and let out a long breath. She headed for the living room and let herself slump onto the couch.

Dad had left the TV on a news channel. Bold colorful images of war violence flashed into our living room like it was happening right in front of us. Faye gasped and I grabbed the remote, shutting it off.

"The world is at war again?"

"It never really stopped," I said wishing I could offer better news. "There's a war going on somewhere in the world all the time."

Faye's face pinched up and I was afraid she might start crying.

"I don't belong here, Adeline," she said. "Can you take me back?"

I understood her emotion of feeling like she didn't belong here. I didn't feel like I belonged here, either. As much as I loved my dad, he and I didn't connect. I felt a stronger bond with Faye than I had with my father.

And, even though Marco was a good friend, and sometimes, like this afternoon, not even that annoying, he didn't stir me like Howard did. Thinking about Howard made my heart twist. I missed him.

Faye wasn't the only one who wanted to go back.

FOURTEEN

"I'VE NEVER TRAVELED before by bringing it on intentionally," I said. "I'm not even sure I can, but I do know it is triggered by strong emotion. Usually anger."

"Anger?" Faye said.

"Yeah, I guess I have a few anger issues. But, fear is also a strong emotion, so maybe that will work."

"How are we going to bring that on? Should I jump out from behind the sofa and go *boo*?"

"No," I grinned. Like that would work. "We have access to something far scarier than that now."

I picked up the remote and clicked the TV back on.

Faye looked slightly amused. "I can't believe you don't even have to get up to turn the television on and off."

"Uh, no. We're pretty lazy that way. And we have hundreds of channels."

She shrugged incredulously. "Of course you do."

I clicked to the pay-per-view channel, and picked the latest horror flick.

"Sorry, to have to do this to you, Faye. You can close your eyes if you want. Just don't let go of my hand."

I didn't like scary movies, and as I expected, I screamed the first time the deranged killer jumped out at the stupid girl wandering in the dark alone. By the time he was on to his next victim Faye and I were hurdling through dizziness and a tunnel of light.

All Faye said was "Whoa", when we were flung back to 1955. We stood in the empty field where my house would one day be built. Faye let out a loud, long sigh, and started speed walking toward town, every once in a while throwing a furtive glance my way.

"Do you want to talk?" I said.

"Um, not yet," she said softly. "Later."

I should have figured this would shake her up. Her change in personality scared me. Her normal take charge, no loss for words self had disappeared. I hoped I hadn't permanently damaged her.

Faye still wore the thin strapped sundress and flip-flops I'd lent her and looked more than a little disheveled. Dressed the way we were I suggested we stick to the back alleys.

She obviously agreed, since she turned into the next one we came upon. It smelled dry and dusty, but with a strong floral scent that wafted from all the backyard gardens. Back yards were interesting and said a lot about the owners.

Some had freshly painted fences with mowed lawns and weeded flower beds and vegetable gardens; others were full of the noise of children and their belongings were scattered everywhere. There were the pet owners, whose dogs were set off to anxious barking escapades as we passed by.

No shortage of garbage pails or beat up cars and trucks, either.

We entered the block where Faye's home was located. Just as we were about to turn into her backyard, I saw the red flashing lights and pulled Faye back sharply, behind the wobbly fence.

"Police," I said.

An old fifties, round hooded, black and white cruiser was parked right behind Howard's truck. My heart jumped. That meant Howard was here. I lowered my voice. "We have to wait until they leave."

"Why are the police here?" Faye said.

"Um, probably because someone reported you missing."

"Missing? Oh, no. Didn't you say that you come and go at the exact same moment?"

I thought I had explained it clearly before, but I guess the whole thing was kind of confusing.

"That's the way it works on that end, when I come and go from my time. When I'm here, time goes by at the usual pace. We were in 2012 for a day and a half, so we were missing from here for that long, too."

"I missed a whole day of salon appointments and my next date with Larry?"

Couldn't really say I was sorry to hear she missed her date.

The door to the house opened and two policemen stepped out. Howard followed and stood with his arm braced up against the door frame. You could really see the definition of his bicep that way. He was so *hot*, I thought I'd melt then and there!

As soon as the police cruiser backed out and drove away,

Faye headed straight for the house. Howard's eyes widened with surprise when he saw us walk out of the bushes.

"Faye!"

She didn't answer him, just squeezed by. He moved before I got there so I didn't get the treat of rubbing past his body. Actually, I was wondering where my greeting was? Howard seemed to have forgotten about *us*.

I closed the door behind me. Howard ripped into Faye. "Suppose y'tell me where ya were? Do y'know how worried I was? I mean I get this call at the vineyard, from Benny saying this guy named Larry was looking for me. That he had to talk to me about you?

"I finally reach him, the connection isn't that good, y'see, and Larry tells me he shows up for a date, and you're not here."

Howard was so intense, kind of frightening, but really attractive at the same time.

"At first I just thought y'were trying to give the guy the slip, so I said, not my problem, but then he went on to say how y'didn't open up your salon, and ladies were lining up at the door.

"I missed work because of this. Rats, Faye. I could've used the money."

Wow. He didn't give Faye a chance to speak. And he still hadn't asked about me. *Hrumph.* What about *me*? I'd been missing, too.

"I'm sorry, Howard." She glanced at me. "I, it was, I didn't... I'm sorry."

Howard finally turned his attention to me. "Did you have something to do with this?"

Maybe?

Faye jumped in. "It's okay, Howard. Adeline couldn't

help it."

"Couldn't help what? Do y'know that the police are out looking for the both of you, right now at this moment while we mess about?"

"I took her to my place, Howard," I said.

This startled Faye. Her eyes warned me not to tell him the truth, which I wasn't planning on anyway.

"I wanted her to meet my father, because you know, he's alone and she's alone..." Well, maybe that part was true. "But he called to say he'd be a day late. So I talked Faye into waiting. She's been working so hard, and I thought she could use a rest."

"Why didn't y'call to tell someone? Why didn't y'cancel your appointments, Faye, or tell Larry ya couldn't make your date. That wasn't very nice."

Think, think. I had to come up with a way to settle Howard down and fast. "She tried, Howard," I said, "but then the phone lines went dead. The power company started digging near our house and accidentally cut the lines, so she couldn't. And then my father didn't arrive when he said he would, so I was worried and begged Faye to stay one more day. It's my fault."

Faye added soothingly, "I'm really sorry you're upset and that y'missed work. I promise I won't do something like that again."

She looked sternly my way when she said that. I knew then and there, that Faye would never leave Howard for me and my dad.

Howard seemed to calm a bit. When the big issue was dealt with he started noticing the little ones. "Why are y'all dressed like that?"

Oh. I thought Faye looked stunning and youthful in the sundress with her bare legs and bare feet, but by the way Howard's eyebrows crept up his tall forehead, I didn't think he agreed. Faye just smiled and said she was tired and had to lie down.

She left me and Howard alone. Finally, he reached an arm out to me. "Com'ere."

I happily complied and let him wrap his strong arms around me and I melted into him. He made me feel so safe. I felt like I really should be here in the fifties with Faye and Howard. I could live without modern conveniences. Who needed a microwave or cell phones? Dad would be fine without me. He'd had a life that barely included me in Cambridge and now he seemed to have his pick of women to keep him company in Hollywood.

If only I could find a way to stay here, to stop the loop.

"You scared me, too," Howard mumbled into my hair. "Don't run off again on me, okay?"

How could I promise that? I really, really wanted to say that I'd never leave his side ever again.

I was desperate to say it, but I knew that was one promise I couldn't keep. I just pressed my face into his chest and swallowed hard.

HOWARD CALLED me at Faye's Salon all excited.

"I just got a call from the Malibu Fall Fair organizer. One of the singing acts he had scheduled for tomorrow called in sick. He wants me to fill in!"

"That's awesome, Howard," I said, sharing his excitement.

"Do you want to come?"

Uh, that was a big YES.

Howard honked when he arrived late the next morning. It was Sunday, so I didn't have to worry about asking for time off work. I ran out and hopped into his truck, nearly dislocating my shoulder as I closed the door. He gave me a quick peck on the lips and I sat close, as close as I could without getting in the way of the prominent shift stick.

Howard had his cool on, but I could tell by the restless way he drummed his fingers on the steering wheel that he was pretty nervous.

It took half an hour to get there along the ocean highway. I was quickly getting used to living close to the Pacific Ocean, taking in the postcard like sites and the invigorating freshness of the saline air. I breathed deeply. With all the beauty around me, and especially the beauty of Howard beside me reaching for my hand, I was insanely happy.

Which was why I loathed bringing up the topic of Leroy. I had a feeling he might show up at the fair today, and I thought Howard would appreciate the heads up.

"Um, I forgot to mention, that you had a visitor while you were up north picking grapes."

Howard's eyes darted my way. "Really? Who?"

"Leroy."

His shoulders tensed. "What he say?"

I squirmed a bit. How much should I tell him? "Well, he said you owed him something."

"Was Faye there?"

"No. I was alone."

He sucked in air and stared at me. "He didn't touch you, did he?"

I swallowed. I wanted to tell Howard the truth because I

was afraid of Leroy and what he might do if Howard didn't sort things out. "No... but..."

"But, what?"

"He kind of threatened to, if you didn't give him whatever it is he wants."

Howard's eyes settled on me. His jaw tightened and his nostrils flared.

"If Leroy ever lays a finger on you, I promise, I'll..."

I was sorry now that I'd brought it up. "He only meant to rile you up. He's not interested in me."

I turned on the radio in an effort to bring back the happier mood. I recognized the tune and started to sing along.

"You have a pretty voice," Howard said. "Maybe you should sing along with me sometime."

"No, thanks. I'm more of a behind the scenes kind of girl." I sighed as I stared out the window, crisis averted.

THE THING I loved the most about life in the fifties was all of the space. Lots and lot of space. And not so many high risers, I mean, a person could see. Malibu Beach had over twenty-one miles of beach, pristine shoreline that ran north and south as far as the eye could see.

I felt a little giddy when I spotted the fairgrounds. The colorful merry-go-round, the Ferris wheel, all the people in pastel fifties wear—it was the candy store filled with all my favorite treats.

We strolled through the grounds, and Howard pointed to the food stands—hot dogs, lemonade, cotton candy, popcorn.

"Would you like some?"

"Cotton Candy, if you'll share with me," I said.

He smiled and paid the nickel (nickel!) for a massive beehive of pink, wispy sugar.

We picked at it as we headed to the stage, me with the cotton candy in hand and Howard lugging his guitar. I waited while Howard got directions from the stage manager; what time he would play, what act he was following.

He left his guitar behind the stage and wrapped an arm around my waist.

"I think I see the gang," he said, motioning toward the stands. I nodded seeing them, too. Benny wore trousers and a UC bomber jacket, Judy was dressed in a soft blue cotton dress and a white scarf over her red curls, and Elmer had his usual arm hold over Judy's shoulders. Judy saw us and waved.

I sat beside Judy with Howard taking the spot on my other side. He immediately started in on gig speak with the boys. Judy turned to me, obviously bored with the guy talk. Elmer let her go to mix in with the boys.

"I love your shoes," she said, gawking. I wore black patent leather ballet flats from the twenty-first century. Probably made in China or Taiwan, and though similar to the flats worn here, there was nothing quite like them around, of course.

"Thanks."

"Where'd ya get 'um?"

"Uh, my aunt from, uh, Sweden, sent them to me." I didn't want to send Judy on a wild goose hunt by suggesting she could get them anywhere near here.

The guys burst out laughing about something and Judy turned to look. I noticed once again that her eyes went to a form leaning against a post on the other end of the stand.

My stomach did a small flip. It was Leroy in his trademark bad-boy, black, leather jacket and permanent frown.

"What's the scoop with Leroy?" I said quietly.

"What? What do you mean?" Judy said defensively.

"I don't mean anything. Just, he seems..." I didn't want to give away Howard's personal issues with Leroy, but I was hoping Judy would "happen" to shed some light. "... I don't know, unhappy."

"He does tend to brood," Judy practically purred.

"You have a thing for him, don't you?"

Her dreamy eyes startled wide. "What do y'mean?"

"Well, I can't help noticing that you tend to look at him a lot."

She gasped. "Oh, no, y'can tell?"

"It's pretty obvious."

She reached for my arm. I turned slightly so her hand would land on my sweater. "No, don't say that! Elmer mustn't know."

"I won't say anything. What's up with you and Leroy, anyway?"

"Nothing's up." She sighed. "That's the problem. I've been sweet on Leroy for forever, but he barely acknowledges me. I agreed to be Elmer's girl because I thought it would make Leroy take notice."

"Yeah, but Elmer seems like a nice guy," I offered.

"Oh, he is. I don't know why, but, I just seem to be attracted to the bad boys."

I looked over at Howard who had managed to find a bottle of beer while I wasn't looking, and puffed on a cigarette. For some reason an image of Marco shot through my mind. I couldn't picture him here. I guess I understood the attraction to the bad boy thing.

"It's so unfair to Elmer," Judy whispered. "I feel so

ashamed."

"Judy, it's okay. You're not the first person to fall for someone you shouldn't." I looked at Howard again and wondered if I had just made a random comment or given a confession.

A pretty blonde dressed in a glittering gold dress got on stage

"That's my cue," Howard said. He kissed me quickly on the cheek and ran off.

My stomach did a flip-flop. I felt nervous for him.

Finally, he entered from stage right. He stood tall, with his guitar slung over his shoulder, taking center stage with full confidence.

"Good afternoon, everyone," he said. I noticed a lot of the girls in the crowd sat up straighter and paid attention. "My name is Howard Walker. This song one y'all know, by Frankie Lyman and the Teenagers."

He strummed his first chord and started singing. His voice was strong, with a warm tone. The song was up-tempo. I recognized it, not this version but the one eventually done by the Beach Boys.

"*Why do the birds sing so gay, and lovers await the break of day, why do fools fall in lo-ove.*"

Why did fools fall in love? I'd swear he stared at me when he sang that! My heart jumped and flipped and my body surged with tingly warmth. He was singing this song for *me*.

My smile stretched widely across my face. I tapped my foot and sang along.

When he finished, the crowd applauded and I jumped up, joining them.

"Great song, huh," Judy shouted. "I think he was singing it to you."

I giggled.

The next song was a slower one. He introduced it saying he had written it himself. I didn't recognize it, and my world slowed down a little. A whisper in my head was asking why? And I realized that I'd never heard of the name Howard Walker before coming here. My mood dropped with a sudden thud. Did Howard make it in the music biz? Did I want to know? Maybe he ended up changing his name. That was a really common thing to do in this era.

The song ended and the crowd applauded again. I brushed those dark thoughts aside, forcing myself to remember the burst of happiness I'd felt just a song ago.

I waited for Howard to rejoin us. Benny was flirting with a girl he'd obviously just met and Elmer had reclaimed his position over Judy's shoulders. Leroy had disappeared from his spot at the end of the bleachers, but I just thought, "good riddance."

When Judy and Elmer started locking lips, I decided to go find Howard myself. He was probably trapped back stage with a group of avid fans and I was just the person to come and rescue him.

I dodged clowns giving balloons to children, a group of girls munching popcorn, and a guy stuffing a hotdog in his mouth. I scooted around puddles of spilled drinks and condiment splats.

Instead of the squealing girls I'd expected, when I turned the corner behind the stage I heard scuffling and cursing. I froze at the sight of Leroy taking a swing at Howard. His fist clipped him in the jaw and sent him flying.

FIFTEEN

"HEY," I SHOUTED. My feet fused themselves to the ground, and I felt useless. If the guys saw me standing there, shocked and bug-eyed, it wasn't enough to end the fight. Howard got up and threw himself at Leroy, shouldering him in the gut. Next, they were rolling on the ground.

"Stop it! Howard! Leroy!" They separated long enough to each get on their feet. Leroy wiped blood from his nose. Howard had a red streak running down his face from a cut above his eye.

"What's the matter with you two?!"

Leroy glanced at me and then pointed a finger at Howard. "We'll finish this later. You owe me." He sauntered off and I ran to Howard.

"Howard, what's going on? What does Leroy want from you?

He brushed me off. "It's nothing. Look, I'll meet ya at the stands, okay?" He disappeared through the door that led to backstage, leaving me standing there alone.

I felt lost. Disappointed. Most of all, I hated that I didn't know what to do. Howard was in trouble with Leroy, and I had a feeling it had to do with money. Most likely a lot of money. The girl in the gold dress exited the backstage area with some guy on her arm. Her eyes settled on me for a fleeting moment, long enough to determine that I wasn't any competition for her, before she giggled and strutted by.

The sign on the stage door said "Talent and crew only," so I couldn't chase after Howard. Instead, I went back to the stands to wait for him, feeling small and abandoned. My happy day had been ruined.

I WORKED ALONE with Faye the next day and spent all my mental strength on worrying. I worried about Howard, and what kind of trouble he was in with Leroy, I worried about Faye and how she still hadn't talked to me about what'd happened between us, and I worried about the annoying niggling feeling the plagued me, that maybe I was in over my head.

During a lull I asked Faye about Howard.

"Do you know if Howard is in some kind of trouble?" I pushed the hair snippets that had fallen onto the checkered floor in a big pile.

"Howard is always in some kind of trouble." It seemed Faye was being purposefully vague.

I shouldn't be surprised; she had warned me. I waited to see if she'd ask me for more info. Faye hadn't been very talkative since our little trip to the twenty-first century.

I scooped the hair up into the trash. "Faye, are you okay? We never really got to talk, you know, about what happened."

Faye paused at the bookwork she had her nose in.

"I don't really know what to say, Adeline. It happened, I can't deny it."

"Are you mad? At me?"

Faye took a cigarette out of her apron and lit it. "Ya, I suppose I'm kinda sore at you. Now that I know how it works, I know y'didn't have to take me with you. It was a choice."

"A bad choice, I know. I'm really sorry, Faye."

She nodded, tapping her ash into a daisy shaped ashtray. "I'm sorry, too. I saw things I shouldn't have seen. I'm disappointed in the future, Adeline. I hope I don't live to see it again."

"Oh, don't say that, Faye!" I wanted to wrap my arms around her and comfort her. The old Faye would've been up to that. This Faye, she had a wall up I dared not cross.

"Anyway, what's done is done." She took a long drag. "I did enjoy meeting your father, though."

"You did?"

"Ya, he seems like a good fella. You should be nicer to him."

I wasn't about to argue with her. "Do you want me to leave?"

Her long pause made me afraid of her answer. Then she said, "No, y'can stay. I may be angry, but I know you're alone here."

Faye reached over to stub out her half-used butt. "But, I'm worried about Howard."

She laughed, not in a way that she thought the situation was funny. More like she found something ironic. "Every time Howard gets involved with a girl, it's most definitely the girl that gets hurt in the end. In your case, I'm not so sure."

"What do you mean?"

"You have something going on." She paused, taking a breath. "This thing that y'do, it could actually hurt my brother. I don't want the same thing happening to him that happened to me. It's not right."

I swallowed hard. I knew what she was asking. She wanted me to end things with Howard.

But, I liked Howard. A lot. I didn't want to do that.

"I'll be careful," I said. It was the most I could offer her. I excused myself and went outside for some fresh air. I felt bad that Faye didn't find me worthy of her brother, but it really hurt that she didn't seem to love me anymore.

THE DAYS WENT on like that: me working during the day for Faye, and Howard sometimes joining us for supper, then taking me out to hang with the gang to drink and smoke cigarettes. Leroy never joined in anymore.

Which was a good thing in my books. Not only did Howard seem more relaxed, Judy seemed to settle into her relationship with Elmer, who, in my opinion, was a much better guy for her.

One night Howard arrived after supper while I was getting ready in the bathroom. I applied a new lipstick I'd bought recently at the general store, Cotton Candy, and smiled. Cotton Candy would always remind me of Howard.

When I headed for the kitchen, I could hear them arguing in muffled tones. I stopped in the living room, out of sight. I knew it was wrong to listen but I couldn't stop myself.

"Faye it's just for a few days. I promise I'll pay y'back."

"That's a lot of money. How do ya plan on paying *that* back? You don't even have a decent job."

"Oh, don't start that with me. Do y'know how much money a guy can make on a hit song? It's just a matter of time for me."

"Everything is just a matter of time with you. Howard, we've been through this a hundred times. You got an inheritance same as me. It represents years of our father's hard work. I can't let ya lose my portion, too."

I heard a bang on the wall, like Howard had put his fist into it. He burst into the living room and on seeing me, he grabbed my hand and pulled me out the door with him.

My throat grew dry and I forced a hard swallow. Howard's anger frightened me. He opened the passenger door and practically pushed me in. When he got in the driver's side he took a deep breath. Instead of starting the truck up and squealing out of the driveway, like I'd expected, Howard reached for me, pulling my face close to his. Then he kissed me hard; with more pent up passion than I knew what to do with.

"Howard," I gasped in between breaths. "What's wrong?"

The urgency in his kisses slowed down. He ran his fingers down the side of my face, sending chills down my back.

"Adeline, I think I love you."

My heart surged with a mix of fear and desire, and I started to tremble. I was dizzy and I knew what was coming next. I had to get away from Howard and quick.

"I'm sorry, Howard." I opened the door and pulled away. "I, uh, heard from my father earlier, and I have to go. I'll come back soon."

I ran off down the dark street. The last thing I heard before the flash of light was Howard calling my name.

SIXTEEN

IT WAS NEARLY impossible to act normal at school the next day. I'd gone back to my house in a daze the night before, barely registering the redhead with my dad in the kitchen. I couldn't stop thinking about Howard. Even in my dreams I couldn't escape him.

I'd never met anyone so passionate before. And, he'd said he *loved* me.

Still, I was torn: a part of me was undeniably attracted to Howard and emotionally attached. But, did I *love* him?

And he wasn't without his problems; that was for sure. But, were they problems I could deal with? Could we deal with them together?

Then, my mind would flip back to the base hotness of Howard—the firmness of his chest, the strength of his arms and the scent of his cologne. Even though I was back at school with the stress of boring classroom lectures, classrooms filled with teen angst and subpar cafeteria food, it turned out I couldn't keep from smiling when I thought about him, especially when

I recalled our last passionate kiss. Bluebell and Marco noticed it too, and said so when we sat together at lunch.

"You're crushing on someone," Bluebell said. "Aren't you?"

I couldn't deny it, even if the massive blush that blasted my face wasn't a big give away. "Yeah, I'm kind of with someone."

"Who?" Bluebell said, confused. "Does he go to this school?"

"No. He's not in school anymore. He's older." It felt good to say that. I was dating someone older than a senior in high school. I felt so mature.

"That was fast," Marco said. The line of his lips pulled downward. "I didn't notice that you had company recently."

"Well..."

"And what about the long distance guy? Does he know?" Then Marco pushed his chair away, got up and left. Just like that.

"Boy," I said slighted by his lack of enthusiasm with my happy situation. "What's his problem?"

"Wow, you're really clue aren't you?"

"Clue?"

"Clueless. Marco is into you."

"No he's not," I said a little too strongly. "We're just friends. You said so yourself. Marco is friendly with everyone."

"True, but I've known Marco for a long time. And as much as I hate to admit it, there's something different about him when he's around you. I'd say he's been smitten with you since the first day you moved to town."

Oh. I guess I was *clue*. Or maybe I wasn't. Maybe I just wanted to be.

The warning bell went and I left for my locker to gather my books for Social Studies. This was one of the classes Marco and I had together. Like usual, he saved me a seat right beside his, but kept his eyes averted as I slid into my chair. I tossed my books onto my desk, letting them fall open and thought about what Bluebell had said.

Had Marco really liked me since the first time he'd seen me. And when was that exactly? Was it when he was peeping at me through my window? Or when Dad and I first drove into our driveway the day we moved in?

Or was it the first time I'd officially met Marco, riding that pink bike.

I faced him. "What did you sell your bike for?"

"Huh?" Though he was leaning away from me, arms folded over his chest, his face was already steered toward me and I realized with a start, that he'd been staring at me.

"When we first met, you told me that you had to ride your sister's bike because you sold yours to buy something else. What'd you buy?"

"My guitar."

Oh. I'd just assumed his mother had bought that for some reason. "That was a good reason to sell it, then."

"I'm glad I have your approval." There was an edge to his voice when he said this.

"What's the matter with you?" I still wasn't convinced that Bluebell's assessment was correct.

Marco leaned toward me. I could smell his fresh soap scent. It made my heart jump a little. A nice change from the smoke and beer smell that lingered around Howard, I had to admit.

"You're lying," Marco whispered.

"What?"

"You don't have a boyfriend," he said smugly. "You like me,

but you're afraid to admit it so you're fabricating a 'boyfriend' to keep it safe."

Did he just *say* that? He really thought I *liked* him? "You're crazy," I sputtered.

"Admit it, you like me and you're afraid."

I shook my head firmly to let Marco know how wrong he was.

"Yes, you are. You're afraid to have a *real* boyfriend. It's easier to make one up."

"You wish, Marco." I couldn't believe what I was hearing. Howard may not be "real" in this time, but I was definitely not making him up.

He leaned back again and grinned. "I don't wish. I know."

Argh. I'd never met anyone so aggravating in all my life. Not to mention conceited and self-assured.

Yet, totally appealing and alluring at the same time. How was that possible?

He smirked at me and I wrinkled my face, scowling back. For some reason, I couldn't stop staring at his lips.

MARCO STAYED BEHIND to skateboard and frankly, I was glad. I didn't think I could put up with his big-headed ego all the way home on the bus.

For some reason the bus was late, which gave me more time than usual to watch the skaters. Actually, it was kind of crazy what they did. I'm not versed in skater culture or lingo, but I was surprised at how athletic they actually were. It was hard to tell with some of them. With their jeans hanging halfway down their butts, it was amazing that they were able to land an "Ollie" or whatever it was called, at all.

Those boys were getting some good air. Quite a crowd gathered to watch, and so I moved in a little closer for a better look. Marco was a pretty good skater, even I could tell that. I guess it must help that he surfed. The way he maneuvered his board, tilting it up and over at his command, making jumps off cement stairwells that made the onlookers gasp. It made me gasp. I almost choked on my heart as he soared through the air off sixteen cement steps and landed to the applause of the crowd. He looked smooth and confident, and yeah, kind of hot.

I wasn't the only girl who thought so, if you could go by the gaggle that jumped up to pat his arm and giggle their appreciation.

He caught me watching him and cocked an eyebrow with a sparkle in his eye. His lips curled into that annoying smirk. Jerk. I turned quickly, not wanting to give him the satisfaction.

LATER THAT DAY, after Dad had left for an evening class, I sat at the kitchen table doing my math homework. I tried to concentrate on integers, but my mind kept going back to Marco and his smug declaration in Socials, to the smug grin he flashed at me while skating, to just his overall smugness. I let myself get so irritated; I got up and put the kettle on for tea.

I did my deep breathing exercises and gathered together all my fond images of Howard. Hunky, cool, mature Howard. I let his dreaminess calm me. The whistle blew and I poured the hot water in my cup, ready to settle back into my homework.

The sound of people shouting erupted outside. I peeked out the window to the street where I spotted Marco and Dan Highland swearing at one another. Dan pushed Marco in the chest. Marco pushed back. Then, Dan took a swing, catching Marco straight in the jaw.

Another fist fight? What was wrong with the guys in my life?

I ran outside at the same time as Candice and Marco's mother, who rattled off something loudly in Spanish. Marco was on the ground, his lip bleeding. I raced to him.

"Are you, okay?"

He nodded, wiping his chin with his hand.

Candice was shouting at Dan and her mother. I couldn't understand a word, but I knew something bad was going down. Marco's mother yelled back at Candice, pointing to the house. Dan Highland got into his car and laid rubber on his way out, the street hockey kids jumping out of the way just in time.

"Oh, my God, Marco," his mother said, coming over. She was dressed for the office in a dress suit and heels. "Are you all right?"

"I'm fine, Mamá."

"That boy is bad news. He better not come around again."

Marco stood up, a bit shaky. I automatically put my shoulder under his arm for him to lean on.

"And you must be Adeline." Marco's mother smiled at me. "Marco has told us so much about you. I can't believe that this is the way we meet."

"Hi, Mrs. Diaz."

"I'm fine, Ma," Marco said. "I know you need to leave."

Mrs. Diaz kissed Marco on the cheek. "Okay, if you think you are fine. I have a meeting I need to go to."

Mrs. Diaz left and I helped Marco to his house.

"What happened?"

"Dan showed up high on something. My mother won't tolerate drugs of any kind. He wouldn't leave when she told him to, so I stepped in. Dan dared me to take it outside and you saw the rest."

"Why does Candice put up with him?"

"I don't know. She thinks she *loves* him. I told her we'd call the cops if he came around again. That's why she's so mad."

When we got to his front door, he looked down at me and grinned. "See, you *do* like me."

"What?" I pulled away, realizing belatedly that Marco hadn't actually needed me to help him walk.

"Oh, you...."

"It's okay, Adeline. I could still use a nurse." He tilted his head flashing me his puppy dog eyes and that insufferable smirk. "Want to come in?"

"I think you are capable of nursing yourself. Good night."

He laughed and then winced, holding his wounded jaw.

I stormed back to my house, fuming. Served him right.

THE NEXT DAY I waited for Bluebell by my locker as our classes were in the same building. I saw her pixie-like form hobble in the distance and refrained from pulling my cell out of my bag to check the time. Instead I thought about Marco and how good he'd looked this morning, all fresh and sporty with just a hint of a tough guy bruise on his chin. He'd grinned as his eyes darted my way while we walked to the bus, like he had some kind of secret insight to my heart.

Funny, his smugness was kind of growing on me.

I snapped out of my Marco daydream in time to see Dan Highland and his gang pass by Bluebell. Dan swaggered ever so slightly to the right, knocking Bluebell into the lockers. If you hadn't been watching at the right moment, you would've thought she just slipped on her brace. She caught my eye and knew I'd seen what happened.

Dan caught my eye, too.

I'd managed to stay fairly invisible so far, the few weeks I'd been at Hollywood High, but I sensed that was all about to change. Dan's eyes never left mine like he recognized me, maybe from the street yesterday when I ran out to stop the fight he was having with Marco.

Worse yet, his mouth curled in such a way to let me know he liked what he saw. I had a flashback of my encounter with Leroy and my knees buckled as I pressed against the lockers.

"Hey," he said. He leaned against the locker next to mine with his arm over my head. "Have we met?"

"No."

"Funny, you look familiar." He grinned at me like I cared. "Anyway, there's a party this weekend." Dan glanced at his buddies who'd circled around us. "You wanna go with me?"

"Don't you have a girlfriend?"

"Nope, not anymore."

By then Bluebell had caught up to me. "Leave her alone," she said. It was like the world started spinning in the other direction—little Bluebell standing up to a thug like Dan Highland.

He started laughing like he'd just whiffed laughing gas and stopped just as suddenly. He poked her shoulder with his finger so hard she lost her balance and fell to the floor again.

"Stay away from me, freak," he said.

Then we winked at me and left with his friends, laughing like he owned the school.

I turned to help Bluebell off the floor, but she shrugged me off, and glared.

"With friends like you...," she spat.

Who needed enemies?

"Bluebell," I said after her as she hobbled by.

"Just forget it." She turned into her class, and I knew I'd majorly screwed up. She hadn't hesitated to stick up for me, but I couldn't bring myself to say one word for her.

MY STOMACH squished together with nerves when I entered the cafeteria at lunch. I wondered if Bluebell would even sit with me. Marco was already with her and he waved me over.

"I got you a tray."

Saved me from standing in line. Marco was thoughtful like that.

"Thanks." I hoped to catch Bluebell's eyes but she kept them averted.

I took a bite of my turkey sandwich, trying to come up with something clever to say to break the ice with Bluebell. Then I remembered the date.

"It's the anniversary of James Dean's death on Sunday."

Marco took the last bite of his sandwich. "Who's James Dean?"

Unbelievable. And here I thought he knew everything.

"You don't know who James Dean was?" I said. Did it really only take one generation to be forgotten?

"He's the guy from the classic movie, *Rebel Without a Cause*," Bluebell said. She didn't look at me while she spoke, but at least she was talking. "It was a big hit because it was one of the first movies about teen angst. I watched it and thought it was kind of weird."

Okay, sometimes I just didn't get these guys. One didn't even know who James Dean was and the other dissed his greatest film.

Marco seemed quieter than usual, too. He stared out the window and I followed his gaze but didn't see anything out of the ordinary. Then he said, "Today could be our last chance to surf."

"Why?" I asked. "I thought surfing went all year."

"It's going to get too cold to go swimming soon, at least without a wet suit which I don't own. Plus, according to the weather channel a storm's moving in tomorrow."

He looked at me. "Do you want to come?"

"Now? What about school?"

"Let's cut."

Bluebell let out a huge sigh, still refusing to look me in the eye. "I'm heading to class." She stood, balancing on her brace. "I'll know what happened if I don't see you guys at the bus."

She left me with Marco, and I'd lost my chance to apologize.

"So...," Marco prodded.

Why was he asking me to cut school? To prove our friend-ship? That I'd do something off center with him?

I should've said no, but I found myself nodding my head. I might not like Marco as more than a friend, but I did want him as a friend.

We took a city bus back to our homes. Both of our parents were out so it was easy to run in, get our swimming suits on and then meet outside.

I wore a string bikini under a sun dress and a light sweater.

I don't know why, but I still wanted Marco to find me attractive, proving I was indeed selfish and vain.

We took the 704 metro bus down Santa Monica Boulevard to the last stop by the beach. My hair blew across my face, and I gathered it up, tying it with a band I'd had on my wrist.

The wind blew the sand in little tornados creating small intermittent sandstorms on the beach that Marco and I had to turn our backs to.

"Ouch," I said. "That stings."

"Yeah, but wind and great waves go together. Look." He pointed to one spectacular wave that looked suicidal to me.

"You're not going out on that, are you?"

"I sure am." He sprung to his feet and jogged over to the board rental place. He didn't bother coming back to drop off his shirt, so eager was he to get in the ocean. He dropped it like a rag just before the water line and ran in.

Marco was a strong swimmer and he had his board out to what looked like the middle of the ocean to me, waiting for just the right wave.

I saw it coming, like a giant wet tongue about to lap up dinner. I stifled a yelp. The wave shot overtop of Marco, and I thought for sure he would be dragged down to the depths never to be seen again, but sure enough, he popped into view, riding his board like a master.

When he got closer to shore I could see clearly how buff he actually was. Strong legs poised over the board just so, and a six pack stomach tensed up for balance and defined biceps and pecs as a result, I guessed, of swimming and hauling around a heavy board.

I hadn't realized how strenuous the sport of surfing was. It certainly did some fine things for Marco.

He skimmed to shore, picked up his board and headed my way. He shook his curls out like a wet dog, and I surprised myself once again by feeling attracted.

He plopped down on the towel beside me, so close I felt his goosebumps against my skin. His eyes met mine and I was mesmerized by how the water dripped off his eyelashes and over his cheekbones.

"I like you, Adeline."

I pulled back a little, surprised he was bringing up this topic again. "Well," I started carefully, "I like you, too."

"But I *like*, like you. I want you to break up with your fake, long distance boyfriend and go out with me."

My heart stopped pumping. Part of me wanted to say yes to Marco. I *did* like him, but what about Howard? I was already into something, whatever that thing was, with him. Being with Marco, too, would be cheating. Even if Howard existed in a different time.

"Adeline?"

I shook my head gently. "I can't."

Marco turned away from me, and stared out at the ocean. "Your imaginary boyfriend has some pull. Not sure I can compete with that, anyway."

"I'm sorry."

"Hey, don't worry about it. I'll just go get a fake girlfriend of my own. We could double date."

He stood and peered down at me. "Enough serious talk. Let's go in."

I looked past him at the waves. "I don't know. It's looking a little rough."

"You said last time that you'd go in," he said. "Come on.

You don't want your first summer to end without having gone in the ocean, do you?"

"Oh, okay, fine." *You whiner.* I slipped off my flip-flops and then climbed out of my sun dress. I felt self-conscious with Marco watching me. A soft smile formed on his face, so I guess I looked all right.

Marco dove in with the grace of a dolphin. He was definitely in his element. I, on the other hand, got wet in increments. Marco laughed and splashed me.

"Hey!" I said with a yelp, then splashed him back.

"Chicken!" he called, splashing me again. "Just jump in."

I splashed him back. "I'll do it the way I want to." Our splashing episode amped up until I was soaking wet. I couldn't help but laugh.

The distance between us grew shorter, the splashing weaker and our laughing reduced to giggles. Before I knew it Marco had me in his arms. Our faces were inches apart and despite the conversation we just had, I was sure he was about to kiss me.

It all happened so fast, I didn't even have time to think that I shouldn't be touching him skin to skin. Especially this much skin!

And, technically, I was with someone else, even if he was from a different time, and Marco knew it. That made me mad, that and the fact that I actually wouldn't have minded kissing Marco. What was wrong with me?

I pushed him away gently, stepping back just as a wave hit us both. It caught me by surprise and I ended up taking a big, salty drink. My feet shot out from under me and I lost my balance, falling underneath the next wave.

I couldn't breathe. The waves were too high and too wild

for me to get my footing again. My heart skipped and plunged and I was encased with the blackness of panic. I was going to drown!

But, I didn't. Instead, something happened that had never happened before. I'd found my footing, the waves suddenly calmed, and stopped splashing in buckets over my head. In fact the tide was at a different level. I caught my breath, coughing and gasping. I searched for Marco, but he wasn't there.

"Marco!" I scanned the area directly in front of me, and then searched the horizon. He was nowhere.

"Marco!" I ran back to the beach, and then stopped short. There were more people here than I remembered. They were dressed very differently, too. More reserved. More fifties-ish.

Oh no. In the midst of practically drowning, I didn't notice the dizziness or the white light. I had traveled.

And all I had on was a skimpy string bikini.

SEVENTEEN

ONCE ON THE SHORE, I borrowed a striped blue and white towel whose owner must have been in the ocean. I dried myself off, arms and legs first then I rubbed the flannel over my hair, all the while trying to register what had just happened.

"Hey, that's my towel!"

So, I was wrong about the owner being out of sight. I offered an apologetic glance, dropped the towel and ran.

Unfortunately, the beach was just as far from Hollywood in 1955 as it was in my time. It felt farther away actually, since there was less urban sprawl.

I felt very exposed, practically naked, and I wrapped my arms around my chest as though that concealed anything, but it did help fight off the goosebumps. I moved as fast as I could in bare feet, wincing as pebbles and stones poked at my soles and got stuck between my toes. I searched for a bus stop, then I remembered that I didn't have any money. It would be a long walk to Faye's, but I couldn't really see another option.

Especially, the one that eventually presented itself. One I would have rather avoided.

A police cruiser pulled up beside me and came to a stop. I kept walking hoping that I wasn't the reason it had pulled over. I was wrong.

"Miss?" the officer called.

I shot him a dubious look. "Me?"

He nodded with a bemused expression and got out of the car. His partner exited the car, too. I tried to picture what I must look like. A teenager, average height, short bleach blonde hair (wet and stringy) with more flesh showing than they'd probably seen in the street before. Why didn't I wear my Speedo one-piece?

"I'm afraid you'll have to come with us," he said, stepping toward me. He had a little wormy mustache that was quivering up and down and a slight pot belly that hung over his belt buckle.

"Why?" I was shivering again and more than a little embarrassed.

"Indecent exposure, miss."

"Indecent exposure?" I squeaked. "I have all my private parts covered up!" Barely, but still. The officer's mustache stiffened, not at all amused.

The second officer opened the door to the back seat. He was clean shaven and hardly looked old enough to be a cop. "We can handcuff you if you resist, it's up to you."

The only thing more embarrassing than traipsing around a police station in a string bikini, would be traipsing around a police station in a string bikini and handcuffs.

My first arrest. I thought maybe I'd get caught stealing or

loitering one day due to my time travel problem, but never did I think it would be for indecent exposure.

The officer swung open the back door, and I crawled into the hot space. The sun beating in through the back window had heated up the vinyl seats, and I made involuntary complaining noises when the bare skin on the back of my legs made contact.

The precinct was a colorless, artless room. The din of noise from talking and the clicking of typewriter keys came to a full stop when I walked in. One of the secretaries jumped up, shuffled through a cupboard door and almost skipped over to me in her sensible shoes. She offered me her sweater, a gray knit thing long enough to cover my butt. I took it gratefully.

"I need it back when you leave," was all she said.

The mustache officer directed me to a chair in front of his desk. It had a stack of paperwork in a metal tray on one end and a gigantic phone on the other.

He pulled a sheet of paper out of his drawer along with a pen. "Name?"

It was times like this that I wished I had a common name, like Jane Smith or Sarah Jones. "Adeline Savoy."

"Got ID?"

I waved my bare hands at him. "Uh, no purse."

"Right. Age?"

Hmm. I'd told Howard I was eighteen and if it got back to him that I wasn't, well, that could complicate things. However, at eighteen I was an adult, and they could throw me in the "slammer." But at sixteen, I was a minor and I'd have to produce parents.

"Miss?"

I'd have to take my chances. "Eighteen."

"Where are your clothes, Miss Savoy."

"The ocean washed them away?"

The officer let out a heavy sigh like I was wasting his time with such a frivolous infraction and that he should be out solving real crimes somewhere.

I couldn't agree more.

He passed the black, bulky phone over to me.

"My one phone call?"

"Just call for a ride home, miss."

Good thing I'd memorized Faye's number, though I had a feeling she wouldn't be too pleased to hear from me.

The phone rang on the other end, and I worried she wouldn't pick up. What would I do then? It wasn't like I had anyone else.

Then, I heard her breathy voice say hello and I let out a relieved sigh.

"Faye, it's Adeline."

"What is it? Are you all right?"

"Well," I turned my back on the mustache officer and his boy-cop partner and lowered my voice. "I'm at the North Malibu Precinct."

"What? You have to speak up. I can't hear ya."

"I'm at the North Malibu Precinct. The jail."

"Oh."

Silence.

"I...sort of...lost my clothes."

"Oh, Adeline."

"I need someone to pick me up."

"As you know, I don't drive. I'll get Howard to do it."

"Thanks, Faye."

I hung up, burning with humiliation and trying hard to ignore all the eyeballs that were peeking my way.

Howard was coming for me. I groaned. What would he think? His girlfriend arrested, off with a warning, for indecent exposure. Boy cop told me to take a seat on a wooden bench by the wall. I pulled the secretary's sweater over my body, hiding as much skin as possible and complied and then promptly started chewing my nails. I ignored the looks of disgust that were sent my way by the other staff and random persons who entered through the front doors and took me for some kind of wanton lady of the night.

Howard showed up twenty-five minutes later. I reluctantly gave the sweater back to the secretary who played with the pearls around the neckline of her dress when she saw Howard walk in the room. She frowned at me with parental-like disapproval.

When Howard saw me standing there with just my string bikini, he stopped and stared. I couldn't tell if he was angry, disgusted, or intrigued. I felt myself flare with embarrassment.

Then I spotted a little upturn of his lips. He called me with the curl of a finger and something squealed inside of me. Wow. I'd follow this man anywhere.

Howard and I stepped outside into the sunshine, and he swooped me up into his arms.

I let out a little yelp. "Howard, what're you doing?"

"I noticed that y'didn't have any shoes on." He carried me to his truck, opened the side door, then gave me a hand to help me in.

"Thanks, Howard," I murmured.

The truck roared to a start, and before Howard shifted into gear, he handed me a paper bag. "From Faye."

Inside was the sun dress and flip-flops I'd lent her. I quickly slipped the dress over my head and put the flip-flops on.

"So, what's the story this time, Adeline?"

I didn't think he was angry. Amused maybe. "I was at the beach, I sat too close to the water and the waves grabbed my shoes and clothes."

"You had your clothes off because..."

"It was hot, and I wanted to go swimming."

"You didn't think anyone would notice y'swimming in your underclothes?"

My bikini looked like underwear to him.

"I didn't think about it." This conversation was pure misery.

"I see." Then he chuckled. "Adeline, I've never met anyone quite like you."

No, I didn't imagine that he had.

FAYE JUST SHOOK her head when we got to her house. "Adeline, what are we going to do with you?" She pointed to her bedroom and I knew she was telling me to get some different clothes on.

I grabbed a change of clothes then parked myself in the bathroom. I took my time showering the salty water off me and getting changed. I dried my hair, my natural curls doing the right Marilyn Monroe thing. I wanted to erase the image of drowned rat from Howard's mind. I could hear that the TV was on and peeked out just to make sure Howard was still there. He was lounging on the sofa, looking as hunky as ever. I suppressed a little surge of glee. Howard had waited for me.

I finished up by applying *Sweet Raspberry* to my lips. When I presented myself, Howard grinned widely.

"You look great," he said. "Though, I didn't really mind the former look, except for that y'took it public." He pulled me to him and kissed me. He didn't seem to mind that I wore lipstick, either, so *take that*, Marco.

"Anyway, I hate to leave ya, but I've lined up some work for the weekend." Before my face could drop in major disappointment he continued, "There's a big party at Benny's place Sunday night. You wanna go?"

I forced a smile. "Sure." I loved that Howard liked to show me off to his friends, I just wished I didn't have to wait two days to do it.

I spent Saturday working for Faye, sweeping hair off the black and white, checkered floor, dusting, and providing coffee to the clients as they gossiped about their neighbors and the latest Hollywood scandals, dropping names like Lucille Ball, Elizabeth Taylor and Eddie Fisher.

The salon phone rang. It was one of those old kinds that looked like a little Eiffel tower. I picked up the cone shape hand piece and held it to my ear.

I spoke into the tower, "Faye's Salon."

"Hi, ya," a chirpy female voice said. "Is this Adeline?"

"Yes."

"It's me, Judy. Hey, me and my pal Martha are going to Curos tonight. Ya wanna come along?"

"Curos?"

"Ya, Curos. The stars hang out there all the time. Ya never know who'll show up there and maybe we'll see someone famous."

It wasn't like I had anything else to do. I said yes and Judy said they'd pick me up at 7:00.

Faye seemed happy to hear I was going out, and not with her brother.

Curos was a famous restaurant in 1955, classy and elegant. Faye made sure I dressed the part, handing me a delicate, slim-line dress.

"This is too nice," I said, when Faye presented it.

"Oh, go ahead. I don't wear it near enough and before you know it, it'll be out of style."

After I'd did my face and hair, I examined my image in the mirror. I looked way older and I wished that Howard was around to see me.

Judy and Martha exuded nerves and I found it rubbed off. Curos didn't really look like much from the outside, but inside was a whole different matter. Heavy drapes lined the walls and hung in overlapping waves over the stage. The tables were a dark, rich wood. We followed a crisply dressed waiter to a table at the end.

I only had the money I'd made from working in the salon, which didn't add up to much, so I'd be sticking with dessert and soda.

"The Thalian Ball was held here a couple weeks ago," Judy said. "I would've loved to have been here for that. James Dean came wearing a tuxedo! Can you believe it? I saw pictures in the *Confidential*—he's the cat's meow!"

She and Martha fanned their faces with their hands in what I'd come to see was the universal sign for swoon-worthy guy.

"No one famous playing tonight," Martha said, checking out the entertainment bill.

"That's why it's half empty," Judy explained. "Otherwise there'd be a line down the street. Still, ya never know who might show up."

A guy with a classical guitar had set up on the stage and started playing. We sat near the back, so it was hard to get a good look at his face, but something about him seemed familiar

"Who's that?" I said.

Martha picked up the sheet of paper with the entertainment posted on it. "Uh, his name is Carl Rodney."

I sat up straight. Carlos Rodriguez, Marco's grandfather?

"You all right, Adeline," Judy said. "You look like you seen a ghost."

I kind of did. I took a sip of soda before saying, "Ya, fine."

Carl Rodney was really good. His finger picking was flawless and the warm notes he produced from the nylon strings of his fat guitar filled the room.

When he finished his set, I heartily joined in with the applause. I was definitely going to get his autograph.

"I have news," Judy said during the break.

Martha put her dessert spoon down. "What is it?"

"Oh, I wasn't going to say anything until I was a hundred percent sure I got in, but I applied to UCLA in the dramatic program!" She let out another "eek," and Martha cheered her on.

"That's wonderful news, Judy. How exciting for you! Does Elmer know?"

Judy's face dropped slightly. "No, not yet. But, I'll tell him if I get in."

I made encouraging noises, forcing my face into a "happy for you" smile. And I was. Except, just when I'd thought I'd made a new friend, she was leaving.

. . .

I SPENT half of Sunday getting ready for Benny's party. It seemed like all I did when I came here lately was party. I wanted to look perfect for Howard when he picked me up. I was grateful to Faye for her generosity and continuing willingness to share her wardrobe with me, and for the fact that she was quite fashion conscious. I picked a dusty blue flared skirt with a fine knit cream sweater top. I added a twisted scarf as a headband to my hair and a string of pearls around my neck.

Howard clucked with approval when he saw me and I suppressed the urge to giggle and squeal. He wrapped me in his arms and kissed me like it had been two weeks since he'd seen me rather than two days.

Benny's house was a sprawling rancher in the same neighborhood as Bluebell's, though now only a few homes dotted the landscape. Flashy, shiny, new fifties vehicles lined the drive, and Howard's old truck definitely stood out. He didn't seem to care. The way he strutted confidently to the front door, you'd think he owned the place.

There were wall to wall people, and you could hardly make out the faces with all the cigarette smoke in the air. My lungs rebelled and I stifled a cough. The décor was fifties chic. All the furniture and fixtures had a faux-futuristic space feel. Though America had yet to visit the moon, everyone was fascinated with the space race, and it came out in fifties design.

The far wall was made completely of glass to showcase the view and also the awesome pool. It was night lit, and already filled with people, laughing and kissing.

"Maybe you should join them, Adeline," Howard said smiling.

"I don't have a suit."

He laughed. Right, that was the joke.

"What do Benny's parents do?" I asked, but my eyes said, *Where'd they make this kind of money?*

"Benny's old man is a movie producer. Benny said there might even be a movie star here tonight."

"Really? Who?" I wondered if I would recognize fifties Hollywood royalty. There was Marilyn Monroe, but I highly doubted she would come, would she? Jayne Mansfield, Dean Martin, John Wayne... the list could go on. I found myself scanning the crowd.

I saw Elmer and Judy huddled on a narrow black leather sofa in the corner and pointed. Howard guided me by my elbow over to them.

Elmer handed Howard a beer. Judy was sipping on a green drink, and her eyes were already getting glassy.

"What's that?" I asked her. She wore a thin, black, satiny number with pearls around her neck, looking very sophisticated and Audrey Hepurn-ish. I suddenly felt frumpy and young in my blue flared skirt. She shimmied over and patted the spot beside her and I sat down.

"Do you want one?" Howard said to me, motioning to Judy's drink.

"Oh, yes, darling," she said, slurring slightly. "These are marvelous. You must have one."

"But I'm not..." I was going to say old enough, but she stopped me by putting her red polished finger to my lip.

"Adeline...." She giggled and took another sip. Howard waved a man dressed as a waiter over who was walking around with a tray full of the same green drinks. He scooped one up for me.

"So, what is it?" I took a sip. It was sweet, yet burned going down my throat. "What's the deal with green?"

"It's in honor of Benny's dad's new movie deal," Elmer said. "It's a cutting-edge science fiction—in *color*. It's called *Forbidden Planet*. Apparently, the sky in the movie is green."

Judy's jaw dropped and her glassy eyes popped open wide. "Oh, my God," she whispered, putting her hand to her mouth. "It's William Shatner."

I followed her gaze and started laughing. Sure enough there he was—a younger, slimmer and yes, I'd admit it, beautiful version of William Shatner. *Was that weird or what?*

He was followed around by a guy with a camera, the old boxy kind you held down by your waist. I assumed William was building his press kit.

He was a chick magnet, that was obvious. The girls were making total fools of themselves, fawning him and flirting. And he wasn't even Captain Kirk, yet!

"Oh, my goodness, oh, my goodness!" Judy was fanning herself. She jumped off the couch and pulled me along.

"Judy!" Before I knew it, I was one of those girls. Well, Judy sure was. I just stood there, and yes, was kind of enamored by William Shatner's charisma.

Flash bulbs went off left and right and I felt blinded. "Let's go, Judy." I went back to our spot in the corner glad that Elmer had stayed to save our spots. Surprisingly, Judy was right behind me.

"Wow, that was amazing," she cooed.

Elmer's face grew serious. "Calm down, Judy, for Pete's sake. It's not like he's the president or something."

She turned to me and whispered, thinking that somehow Elmer couldn't hear her, "He's just so handsome!"

"Well, yeah he is now," I said, feeling sorry for Elmer. And maybe because I'd already finished half my drink, I didn't think about the next thing I said. "But, he gets old and fat. All that beauty, *psfft.*" I made a noise like a balloon losing air. I didn't think anything of it until I felt everyone staring at me.

"What?"

"How can you know that?" Judy spit out. "And it was a really mean thing to say. I mean, you don't even know him."

"No, I didn't mean..." What could I say? I took another sip of my green drink and swallowed. All the hubbub over William Shatner followed him outside to the pool deck.

Benny spotted us and sashayed over. "Hey," he said conspiratorially to Howard who had rejoined us. "Gotta game going in the back. You in?"

Oh, no. Poker. Howard nodded. I grabbed his arm and whispered in his ear, "Do you think that's a good idea? Maybe you should stay with me."

He gave me a withering look, then said, "It's just for fun. I won't be long." He emptied his beer and followed Benny out of the room. Elmer got up and ran after them. "I'm in, too."

"Men," Judy said.

Maybe it was just fun for some guys, I thought, remembering the argument Howard had had with Faye. A fuzzy ball of worry rolled around in my gut. I had a sinking feeling it was more than just about the fun for Howard.

The waiter walked by again, and Judy called him over, taking two drinks.

"I don't know," I said, thinking one was probably more than enough.

"Oh, Adeline. Stop acting like such a child. You don't

smoke, you don't drink, you make me feel like I'm hanging out with my little sister."

Okay, that hurt. I knew I shouldn't care what she thought, but I did. I finished my first drink and started on the second.

I knew it was a bad idea when my head started spinning and my tongue and lips felt so fat, I could barely talk.

All the noise and smoke was starting to get to me. Judy wasn't looking so hot anymore, either. Her makeup had smudged around her eyes, her lipstick faded, and her hair was pressed up on one side as a result of her holding her head up with her hand.

"Maybe we should go," I mumbled. "Let's find Howard and Elmer and get them to take us home." I hoped that they were more fit to drive than Judy and I were.

Judy knew where the back room was since she'd been to Benny's before. She tottered down a twisting hallway in a very unattractive manner, and I could tell I was doing the same thing.

We walked into the room just as Howard scooped up the chips from the middle of the table. He had a big grin on his face, with a half burned cigarette hanging out of one side. To my surprise, Leroy was among the six players. His scowl was etched even deeper into his face, if possible.

Then he got up and shoved the table. "You cheated, Walker!"

"I did not." Howard stood abruptly, shifting the table forward. "I won it fair and square. We're even."

Leroy obviously disagreed since in two seconds flat he had Howard on the ground, pounding his face with his fists.

"Howard!" I squealed like a little mouse.

In my fuzzy state of mind, everything felt like it was

moving in slow motion. Leroy threw punches while Howard covered his face, Benny and Elmer pulled Leroy off, pictures fell off the wall, and an extremely distressed blonde ran into the room, shouting, "James Dean is dead!"

Those were the magic words because everyone and everything stopped—the fighting, the yelling, the moving around. Just stopped.

Someone said, "How do you know that?"

"I just heard it on the radio! It's true. James Dean is dead! Died in a car crash on Route 466!"

I could hear wailing coming from outside the room.

Judy dropped into a chair and joined in, sobbing loudly, her mascara tracking black lines down her cheeks. I felt a little odd, being the only one not truly affected by this news as I stood like a statue in the middle of the room. Even the guys looked shook up as they noiselessly righted chairs and sat down.

I imagined that they were feeling the way I'd felt when I'd heard that Michael Jackson had died.

Howard, who was off the floor now, saw me standing there and waited. He probably was wondering what my response would be, if I was about to burst into tears. Nothing. No emotion.

He started laughing. Laughing!

"What?"

"I should have known. Nothing shakes you up. You're somethin' else, Adeline." He walked over to me and kissed me. "Let's give these guys room to mourn."

Howard took my hand, led me back through the house, and past the kitchen. I still felt woozy from those two green drinks and I stumbled a bit. I wondered where he was taking me.

He pushed open a door. It was a bedroom. All my nerve endings started shooting off. I'd have to be the stupidest girl in the world not to understand what Howard wanted.

The room was dark, with only the glow of a streetlight shimmering in the window. Howard pressed in to kiss me. He had the same urgency he'd had the time he'd kissed me after the first fight he'd had with Leroy. Howard liked to transfer his anger into passion. I wasn't sure how I felt about that.

"Hey," I said, "I think you should take me home."

"I'll take you home baby, later." He slurred his words a little and I realized that I wasn't the only one who'd had too much to drink. He kissed me harder, pushing me toward the bed.

"No, really, Howard, I'm not feeling well." By now my legs were pressed up against the bed and it took little effort for Howard to push me over.

"Oh, don't play hard to get, Adeline," he said between kisses. "You said you'd be my girl. C'mon. I love you."

Then, his hand reached up under my sweater. I grabbed hold of his wrist and pulled his hand away. I pushed him off me, and sprinted to the potted plant I'd spotted in the room. I heard myself wretch.

Oh, man, I couldn't believe I'd just vomited in front of Howard. The funny thing was I felt relieved. It gave me a way out. I wasn't ready to give Howard what he wanted.

Howard sat up and stared at me. My eyes were fully adjusted to the dark. I tried to read his expression. Frustration? Anger?

I know what he saw on my face. Immaturity. Fear.

He ran his hand through his hair. "How old are you, really?"

"Sixteen." I squirmed. "And a half." Like that made a difference.

"Oh, Adeline." He let out a big breath. "Look, I'll meet you out front and take you home, okay?" Then he got up and walked out of the room, leaving me alone in the dark.

And I knew that was it. It, whatever *it* was, was over. He'd said he loved me, but he didn't really love me. He just said what he thought I wanted to hear.

I was surprised at how much it hurt, and not surprised that this event triggered the dizziness and tunnel of light.

I was so caught up in the dark emotion of losing Howard that I had totally forgotten the situation I had left in the present.

Suddenly, I was underwater. I gagged and choked, thrashing my arms around wildly. I didn't know which way was up; the waves kept me tumbling like a wet rag in the dryer.

My lungs were bursting and I thought, *this is it*. This was how I died. I got my heart broken and then I drowned in the ocean. I grew limp.

Something tugged my arm and pulled. Next thing I knew I was laying on my back in the sand and Marco was breathing into my mouth.

I sucked in air deeply, and Marco rolled me to my side, where I promptly threw up. Nice. I'd upchucked twice in less than half an hour, in front of two different guys. I was so hot.

"Adeline!" Marco said, clearly worried. "Are you okay? Can you breathe?"

I choked out more water and moaned.

"Adeline."

It took only moments for me to register what had happened. I was shivering in the sand, in the stupid string bikini—which thankfully I had knotted tightly—totally embarrassed to have thrown up in front of Marco, who'd just saved my life.

"Yeah, I'm breathing." My voice shook. Feeling stupid I tried to sit up, but I was all wobbly. Marco propped me up against him so I wouldn't pitch over. He grabbed his towel with one hand, shook the sand out of it and wrapped it over my shoulders.

"What happened out there?" Marco said, his face twisted with concern. "You scared the daylights out of me."

"I don't know. I just lost my footing and the waves tumbled over me and I couldn't get up."

Marco closed his eyes and took slow deliberate breaths. His wavy hair dripped water down his cheeks. His lips were full, open slightly. Boy, he was cute. Not movie star handsome like Howard, but cute. And safe.

And I'd just puked in front of him. I was such an idiot.

Marco was pretty silent on the bus ride home. It wasn't everyday he had to save the life of a friend, thinking that maybe he was too late and you were already dead.

Plus, watching her throw up was likely no highlight.

"I'm sorry I made you go in," he said. He really did look remorseful, and something in me wanted to give him a big reassuring hug, but I resisted. I wasn't sure if it was because I didn't want to hurt Marco by making him believe I might like him, or if it was because I could still smell the stench of vomit in my hair.

"It's not your fault. I can swim, I told you, and I wouldn't have gone in if I didn't want to. You must know me well enough by now to know that. It was just one of those weird freak accidents."

He walked me from the bus stop to my door, still worried. "Are you sure you're all right? Maybe you should get a doctor to check you out."

"I'm fine."

He nodded and turned to leave.

"Marco?"

He glanced back at me. "Yeah?"

"Thank you."

He smiled. "I'd save your life any day, Adeline."

EIGHTEEN

THE WEATHER SYSTEM that threatened to hit southern California came in with a mere sneeze and sniffle. I was beginning to wonder if the weather here would ever be anything but smog and sunshine. I sat out on our patio working my way through a frothy cappuccino and let the sun massage my face. I'd finally awakened after a serious coma-like sleep-a-thon. I'd told Dad I was sick and I must've looked it, since he didn't even try to persuade me to go to school. He even peeked in before he'd left for his acting class to see if I was still alive.

Of course, I couldn't help replaying the events of the previous day, a day that may go down as the worst day of my life. Okay, maybe that was melodramatic, but let's just say, yesterday sucked.

My thoughts went back to Cambridge, to a day when a tall girl with wild, curly hair had chased after me while I was on my way to the bus stop, just after I had traveled back from Cambridge in the fifties.

She claimed to be a time traveler, too. I couldn't believe I hadn't taken the time to talk to her more. How I'd love to have someone to compare notes with now. Anybody with half a sense would've seen the value in at least getting her name. Bluebell would attribute my short-sightedness to my apparent inability to be a proper friend. Marco would craft a wise, analytical personality assessment along the lines of my need to ensure self-preservation or some other rubbish.

I saw movement next door. Mrs. Bradshaw's caregiver held Mrs. Bradshaw's arm as she stepped cautiously out to her table on the patio. Mrs. Bradshaw had large, trendy sunglasses on to cut the glare along with a wide brimmed hat. I waved.

She smiled and with a shaky right hand, beckoned me over. I decided to go. Marco wasn't due back from school for another couple hours, and I had no idea when dad would return so it wasn't like I had anything else to do. Plus, I was starting to feel kind of lonely.

"Hello, Mrs. Bradshaw," I said as I pulled up one of her patio chairs.

"Hello, dear," she said with a stilted shaky voice.

"How are you today?"

The caregiver returned before Mrs. Bradshaw could attempt a response. She brought a tray with a teapot, cream and sugar, and on seeing me there, she left to get a second teacup.

"Hello," she said. "I'm Melissa. I'm Mrs. Bradshaw's niece."

"Nice to meet you."

"I have to run to the pharmacy for my aunt. I'll be back in twenty minutes. Do you mind? I mean, I can leave her alone for short sprints, but I'd feel better if someone were here. I have my cell if you need to call."

"Sure. I'll stay until you get back."

Mrs. Bradshaw wasn't much for words. Her left side drooped from the stroke. I thought the way she slurred her words slightly embarrassed her, and maybe that was why she didn't like to talk.

"Turned out to be a nice day," I said, pouring for both of us. I used double cream and sugar. Mrs. Bradshaw's right hand shook as she took a cube of sugar. I quickly helped to pour the cream.

She nodded again, and I gathered that it was going to be a one-sided conversation for the most part. I wished now that I hadn't agreed to come over. So much silence was awkward and I wasn't used to hanging out with old people.

"I hear you've lived here a long time," I said after a while. "You must like it."

Mrs. Bradshaw nodded carefully. I could see her watery eyes through her sunglass lenses. They never left me and the way she stared made me nervous. I checked my phone for the time. I'd only been here for ten minutes. How long did Melissa say she'd be?

I scanned the street for signs of her car, and that was when I saw Marco's familiar form rolling toward us on his skateboard. My heart jumped a bit, and I was surprised by the joy I felt in seeing him.

"Marco!" I called.

"Hey, Adeline. Hi, Mrs. B."

"You're home early," I said.

His eyes latched on to mine. "I was worried about you. Are you okay?"

"Yeah, I'm fine. Really." I smiled to encourage him. "Especially now that I've slept most of the day."

"That's good."

"Do you want to join us?" I asked eagerly. A third party would get the conversation going. Plus, it could kick start our friendship again after yesterday's humiliation. And, I found, I really wanted his company.

He shook his head and I felt the disappointment weigh heavy like cement shoes. "Sorry, Adeline, something's come up at home." His eyes lingered on my face for a moment. Maybe he was making sure I was indeed okay. Or maybe he'd just invented an excuse so he wouldn't have to hang out with the vomit queen.

He tucked his skateboard under his arm. I watched his back as he left, and noticed a droop in his shoulders. Something wasn't right.

Had I lost Marco and Howard in one fell swoop?

I swallowed hard when I thought of Howard and Faye. Would I still be welcomed at Faye's home now that Howard and I were, well, no longer an item. Would he still drop by if I stayed there? That might be too uncomfortable. Maybe I'd have to figure out different arrangements now.

If only I had listened to Faye, I wouldn't have to worry about being homeless next time I traveled. She had warned me about Howard.

Mrs. Bradshaw must've seen my sadness. She reached over and rubbed my arm, which thankfully was covered by the sleeve of my sweater. "It's okay," she said softly.

I offered a limp smile and took a sip of tea. "What do you think of Marco?" I asked her.

She smiled her crooked smile and nodded. "Nice boy."

Yes, he was a nice boy. That *was* the problem. Marco was just too nice for me.

.   .   .

MARCO BARELY BROKE a smile the next day on the way to school. He avoided my eyes staring off into the distance. I must've totally turned him off with my vomit fest. Plus I'd rejected him. I was such an idiot. My brained swirled over and over trying to figure out how I could undo that damage.

The thing was, I'd changed my mind—did a total round about. My eyes were finally opened. I was into Marco, and I needed to set the record straight and soon.

If it wasn't already too late.

I searched for him at lunch but Bluebell was alone at our usual table. I wondered if she was still mad at me.

"Hey," I said. When she didn't tell me to go fly a kite, I pulled a chair and sat down.

"You notice anything weird about Marco?" I said.

She raised her pierced eyebrow at me. "Yeah, something's off."

"I wonder if it's me?" I whispered. "We had this, uh, thing happen at the beach on Friday."

"Oh my God. Don't tell me he kissed you?"

The way her face crunched up, you'd think that would be the worst thing in the world that could've happened to Marco.

"No, he didn't kiss me, but why would that be so bad?"

"Well, there's your boyfriend, for starters."

"Oh, him. He's not..."

Bluebell tossed me a look. "Real?"

I didn't feel like getting into my issues with Howard.

"I threw up."

"You threw up?"

"Shh, could you keep it down? The whole school doesn't have to know."

"What happened?"

"It's no big deal; I just swallowed a barrel of sea water."

Bluebell snorted apple juice on the table. "You think Marco's avoiding you because you grossed him out?"

"Maybe."

"I doubt that. You know, Adeline, maybe it's not about *you* at all. Ever thought of that?"

We were interrupted by the sound of a chair scratching across the floor and Marco sat down. My face flushed with mortification that he might've overheard our conversation.

If he had, he covered it up well.

"What gives?" Bluebell said.

The vain part of me had wanted it to be about me. He wasn't grossed out by the smell of vomit. In fact, the whole near-drowning incident just made me more vulnerable and enduring, and he wouldn't be happy until we were together so that he'd always be around to protect me. That would shut Bluebell up.

Bad ego, bad.

"My mom wants to move."

"What?" Bluebell and I said at the same time. "Why?"

"She's got a new job opportunity, but it's in Orange County."

"Ooh, that tote sucks," said Bluebell.

My mouth dropped. This was not at all what I'd expected.

"And," Marco said, letting out a long breath. "There's a new man involved."

I felt sick. When I first met Marco, I couldn't stand that he lived right next door. Now, I couldn't stand the thought of him leaving.

"When?" I asked softly.

His gaze settled on me. "October first."

"That soon?"

He nodded. "I've met the guy, and he's a jerk. I don't know what Mom sees in him."

"Maybe she sees the new job," Bluebell said. "She's probably thinking about you kids, you know, how the extra money could really make a difference for you."

Marco scoffed. "That's what she said."

"There's got to be something we can do," I said, feeling hopeless.

"Pray that she sees what a creep this guy is before it's too late," Marco said.

Suddenly, I wanted to throw myself at Marco, wrap my arms around him and comfort him the way he had when I had my breakdown in his room. I imagined the look of horror that would cross Bluebell's face if I did that, not to mention the shock and awe of the whole cafeteria.

And of course, I wasn't entirely sure Marco would appreciate it anymore. I held myself back.

Marco slapped his thighs with his hands and got up to leave.

"Marco?"

He turned and his caramel eyes softened when they met mine. "Yeah?"

"I'm sorry." For everything.

I ACCIDENTALLY SLEPT in the next morning, so Dad drove me to school. And because I didn't get breakfast, we went through a drive-through donut place, where Dad ordered us both caramel lattes and a cream donut.

Though driving with my dad beat taking the bus, I missed my morning time with Marco.

And I missed Marco.

Basically, I had to accept that I'd totally screwed up the only two real friendships I had here. You know what they say: Be careful what you wish for. I wanted a loner life, and well, it looked like I got it.

It turned out that I didn't have any classes with Marco today, so the most I could hope for was a distant sighting, which hadn't happened yet. I had a nervous thought that maybe Marco hadn't come to school for some reason. I'd have to check his house later.

I sipped my coffee and took a bite of my donut sliding the rest back in the little brown bag

When I got to school I tossed my empty coffee cup and I grabbed my books for my next class from my locker. I still had my uneaten donut and flung the bag on top. Though my heart hurt, my stomach still insisted on me paying it some attention, even if it was a not-so-good for you donut.

I turned the corner heading for my next class when I saw something that made my blood boil. Dan Highland bumped into Bluebell again and her brace clanked against the locker door as she fell to the ground.

This time I called out, "Hey!" Dan and his gang turned around, and my brain skipped a beat, like I was watching a movie scene in slow motion.

A slimy grin crossed Dan's face when his dark as coal eyes registered that he knew me.

"Right," he said, stepping into my personal space. "You, me, the party. I didn't forget."

"Yeah, well, don't forget this either." I smudge my half

eaten donut in his face. "Pick on someone your own size, pea brain."

Dan's face froze and I let out a small gasp. I couldn't believe I actually *did* that. I mean, I imagined myself *dreaming* about doing something like that, but not actually doing it. My heart drummed loudly in my ears.

Dan's boys went "*whooo.*" Dan wiped his face with the back of his hand and then pressed in close to my cheek.

"You and me." He made his voice go all deep and husky. "We'll have breakfast together later."

My lips moved and I heard my breathy voice. "Dream on."

"Hey, kids." A teacher clapped his hands in the hall to break things up. "The bell's gone. Get to class."

Dan Highland walked away and started laughing. I was glad he thought it all a big joke.

I stretched out a shaky arm to help Bluebell up.

"You didn't have to do that," she said, dusting herself off.

Yes, I did.

Her class was the next door to the right and she walked in without looking back.

I'd hoped facing up to Dan and helping Bluebell out would make amends in our friendship. It looked like it might be a little too late for that.

A long sigh escaped my lips as I headed for class amazed at how quickly I'd screwed everything up already, and not even a student at Hollywood High for a month yet.

I felt a strong arm tug me into an empty, short hallway. The bell rang and the echoes of the classroom doors clicking shut reached me and my captor.

I gulped as I stared into Dan Highland's intense, humorless gaze.

His nose almost touched mine. "Hey, Baby. I thought we could get the party started early."

I wiggled to get out of his grip. "Let go of me!"

"Ooo, a feisty one. I like 'em feisty."

"You're making me mad, Dan Highland, and you won't like me when I'm mad."

His head tilted back in laughter. "Quoting popular culture? So funny."

I stared at the grip he had on my bare arm as the dizziness started.

"I'm not trying to be funny. Let go of me or you'll be sorry..."

Next thing I knew, I was staring in the blanched out face of Dan Highland.

"Did you feel that?" he said. "Was that, like, an earthquake?"

He'd finally let go of me and I stepped into a busy hallway filled with kids dressed more like me than Dan.

A school banner hung overhead, *Class of 1955*.

My head swiveled back to Dan Highland. I felt like I was watching a traffic accident as it was happening, my heart pulsing with disbelief. I'd brought the school bully back in time. Great.

"What's going on?" he said, his voice suddenly small.

I had little sympathy. "I told you, you'd be sorry."

I didn't know what I was supposed to do about him. I wanted to leave him to fend for himself. If he hadn't been pushing Bluebell and me around between classes he wouldn't be here. I could ditch him and let him sweat it out for awhile.

But, that wouldn't be nice. Or responsible.

Two characteristics I was trying to improve upon.

I peered into the hallway taking in all the angora sweater and saddle shoe wearing girls. The guys streaming through the hall all looked like cookie cutter images of one another, too. Narrow legged Levis, T-shirts with cuffed sleeves, hair slicked back in a "duck bill."

I focused in on Dan's befuddled expression. "Follow me," I said. "And if I were you, I'd pull up my pants."

NINETEEN

I TRIED TO WALTZ through the crowd un-noticed but that worked for all of ten seconds.

"Let's meet at *Biffs* after school for a coke," a girl with cat-eye glasses said to her friends. They all had pageboy haircuts and flared poodle skirts.

Before anyone could respond, they saw us. Their eyes scanned me first and landed on Dan. The din of chatter grew increasingly quiet.

I at least sort of looked the part. I had a similar cut skirt and my Marilyn Monroe hair, though my shoes and blouse weren't quite right for the era

Dan, on the other hand, with his baggy pants sitting low on his hips, the pant legs crumpled like elephant skin over the top of his fat skate shoes, and his messy windblown hair, you'd think he was an alien come to Earth.

And the way the people in the fifties loved their alien theories I wouldn't doubt the rumors would be flying.

One of the guys strolled by with a gang of boys behind

him. He had a black, leather bomber jacket on, much like the
one Leroy always wore, with the collar standing up. I got a bad
vibe off him. He was like Dan's fifties equivalent.

Great. Two Dan Highlands. That was all I needed.

He stopped to scowl. "You guys aren't from our school.
What'cha doing on my turf?"

Kids in the fifties were very territorial—if you could go by
the movie *Rebel Without a Cause*. He probably thought we
were spies from the rival school or something.

I tugged on Dan's sleeve. "We need to get out of here."

Because it was the same school, just newer, we knew our
way around. We managed to skirt around the girls, bumping
past a startled teacher and get out the door onto North Highland Drive. The fifties thug and his gang chased us to the
school boundary. We were literally saved by the bell when the
school buzzer went and they gave up the chase to get back to
class.

Once the threat of getting pummeled to death was gone,
we stopped under the shade of a palm tree to get our breath.
The school "skyline" looked different in the fifties. The library
was now the auditorium. No murals to be seen anywhere.

Dan had his hands on his bony hips and stared down at me
with his dark, steely eyes.

"What is going on here, Adeline Savoy?"

I'd admit I was shocked to hear him say my name. I didn't
think he knew it.

My eyes moved to the traffic flowing past us on the street, a
stream of Fords and Chevy's made in the forties and fifties.

"It must be obvious by now," I said.

He shook his head. "This is crazy. It looks like, *feels* like,
we *time traveled*. But that's nuts? Right?"

What could I say? It bugged me that Dan Highland, the one guy in the world I could easily hate, now knew the most near and dear secret of my life. But the evidence was clear. There was no way I could get away with lying.

"Unfortunately, it's true."

I spun on my heel and headed west on Hollywood Boulevard. I hadn't traveled this far away from my house before, so I was farther away from Faye's than usual. It would be a good hour hike to get there if not more.

I wasn't even sure if I'd be welcomed back, but I didn't know where else to go.

"Wait!" Dan ran after me. "What about me?"

"*You* shouldn't be here!" I spit my words out wishing they were arms that could push Dan around like he did other people with his body. Dan Highland! I still couldn't' believe it.

"But I am here; wherever here is."

I kept walking and Dan was like a dog on my heels.

"This is just so crazy! Are you seeing this? We're in the *fifties*."

"I *know* that."

"What? Is this like a regular gig for you?"

I said nothing. I didn't need to answer to him. As far as I was concerned, Dan Highland was on a need-to-know basis."

"Adeline?"

I felt a tug on my sleeve.

"Look, I know we got off on the wrong foot..."

"Are you kidding me?" I shook a finger in his face. "You pick on kids with physical challenges. I mean, how lame is that? You were forcing yourself on me in the hallway!"

"Yeah, okay. I see how that comes off bad."

"Badly."

"Right, so now you're the grammar queen?"

"I'm not anything to you."

I was becoming the spin-away-on-your-heels queen. I resumed my speed walking pace wanting to distance myself from Dan.

He ran up beside me. "Okay, you're mad. I get it. But what am I supposed to do now?"

"You're a big boy. You figure it out."

"Fine." He stopped suddenly "You're right. See you around."

I flicked a hand not even looking back.

I was relieved to be rid of him for about ten minutes and then I started to fret. What if something happened to him? He wasn't the sharpest tool in the shed as they say. He could get into a load of trouble. What about when I felt the trip back coming on? As much as I despised the idea, I needed Dan to be nearby so I could grab him.

I paused by a small convenience store and wished I had money to buy a coke. I was parched, but all my money was tucked away in a secret place at Faye's.

I was about half way to her house. My choice was to keep going or turn back to find Dan.

My throat scratched and my tongue felt rough and thick with thirst. I wanted to keep going to Faye's, really wanted to, but instead I heaved out a long sigh and turned back toward the school.

I wished I'd never met Dan Highland.

I thought he'd be easy to find. He didn't exactly blend in and now that I was scouting for him, I grew increasingly frustrated when he didn't materialize.

I finally made my way back to the school so I at least could stop off at a water fountain, which I did and slurped backwater like a camel. I scooped a little water into my hand and wiped the sweat off my face.

Anxiety spun a web in my gut as my worry for Dan grew. I'd made a big judgment in error by setting him loose, and I felt angry that this dumb boy was causing me so much extra trouble. Like my life wasn't complicated enough.

An image of Marco flashed through my mind. What if I'd accidentally brought him back with me instead of Dan?

How would I feel, then?

I thought Marco would be cool with my secret life.

Maybe.

You never did know what would set people off. Look at Faye. She didn't exactly appreciate her field trip.

I dodged a teacher as I slipped outdoors to the field where the football team was practicing and a bunch of girls sat on the bleachers watching. If it weren't for the difference in clothing styles, it would look and sound much like a practice from my time.

For some reason I turned down the alley behind the school. Scuzzy alleys and Dan seemed like a good fit.

My instincts proved me right. I heard the scuffle and shouts before I saw the source.

I ran past a large garbage bin, then froze.

Dan was encircled by the guys we'd seen in the hallway earlier. One guy had him in a neck hold while the leather-jacketed leader curled his fist.

I screamed just as his fist connected with Dan's face.

TWENTY

THE THUG GOT one more blow to Dan's stomach before I threw myself in between them. I didn't think it through ahead of time. It wasn't like I was a big, beefy girl who had any hope of stopping a back alley fight on her own.

The guys let go of Dan and he dropped to the ground holding his gut and gasping for breath.

I took careful, slow steps backward.

"You take one move toward me and I'll scream," I said. Not that my screams would be heard through the noise from the sports field. Still, threats were my only weapon. The leather jacket guy smirked.

"Seriously. I'll run for a teacher, I swear."

Wow, even to my ears the threats sounded weak and stupid.

"Hey, Eddie," one of the shorter guys said to the leader. "Let's go, hey. I'm hungry."

Eddie still rubbed his fist. His eyes scanned me up and down and I couldn't help but shiver.

He offered a smarmy smile. "Sorry we beat up your boyfriend."

"He's not my boyfriend."

"Well, in that case." His eyebrows jumped eagerly. "We'll see you later, doll."

Yup, Dan's fifties twin.

Good thing Eddie's stomach was in charge, otherwise Dan and I could've been in deep trouble.

I helped Dan off the ground. His lip was split open and bleeding.

"Let's go to Faye's," I said. "We'll get you cleaned up."

IT FELT like it took us forever to get to Faye's and I was just glad that Dan didn't need to lean on me to walk or anything.

Not that he was disgusting physically. He was actually kind of good looking if you could get past his personality flaws.

Which I couldn't.

Now that we were almost at Faye's I had a new worry.

What if Howard was there?

Not only was I not prepared to see Howard again, I definitely wasn't prepared for him to see Dan. Or see me with Dan.

Not to mention how I would explain Dan to Faye. I could just imagine her eyes squinting in disapproval at another obvious careless act on my part.

Thanks for nothing, Dan.

I decided to approach her house through the back alley, and hide Dan on the back porch, counting on the fact that Faye would be busy in the salon at the front.

The screened in door to the back porch squeaked a little. I stopped, then opened it the rest of the way very slowly.

I motioned to my made-up cot. "Take a seat," I whispered. "I'll be right back." I gave him a second, sterner look. "Don't move."

I slipped in the back door and a wave of weirdness hit me. Not just because I was back at Faye's, but because I felt like I was breaking and entering. I tiptoed to the bathroom. At the very back under the sink was an empty Kotex feminine napkin box I'd pulled from the trash. It was where I kept the money I made from Faye. Maybe not the most secure place to hide cash, not like there was a lot in there, but I thought it would throw off most would-be burglars, especially of the male variety.

I pocketed a few bills.

After taking a long drink of water, I filled the glass for Dan. I grabbed the few first-aid supplies I needed and quietly made my way back to the patio.

"Here," I said. I handed him a wet cloth for his lip and some antiseptic-type cream. He took the cloth and reached for the glass of water. He emptied it and handed me the glass without saying "Thank-you."

"You're welcome," I said anyway. Even though there was plenty of room, I didn't want to sit on the cot beside him. Instead, I leaned up against the patio frame.

"So what's next on the agenda," Dan finally said.

"I'm not sure." I plucked the bills out of my pocket and handed them to him.

Dan examined the old notes. "Cool."

"Yeah, well, the other kind will get you arrested."

Dan lay down and closed his eyes. I immediately regretted

not taking the space when I had the chance. I didn't want him to get comfortable.

"I just can't believe this is true. I'm going to go to sleep okay? This will be over when I wake up, right?"

I pushed his shoulder. "Get up! You can't sleep here. I gave you enough money to get something to eat and find a hostel somewhere."

He sat up and swung his feet to the floor.

"How long will we be here? We will get back, won't we?"

"Yeah, we'll get back." Somehow.

I had an idea. "Wait a minute," I said.

I stepped softly to the table with the house phone. I found a paper and pen and wrote Faye's number on it.

Outside I handed it to Dan. "Phone me tomorrow. Try not to get into any more fights in the mean time. Go for the hobo look."

"Adeline?" Faye's voice reached me from across the living room. Her work day must be ending. "Is that you?"

I pushed Dan's shoulder even harder and hissed. "You have to leave now! Go, quickly. She can't see you here."

I was actually surprised when he popped up off the cot and slipped out the patio door around the corner and out of sight.

Just in time, too. Faye's face poked through the back door. "It is you."

I tried to wipe the anxiety of my face. "Hi, Faye. I didn't want to bother you, but I don't know where else to go."

"Oh, honey." Faye's head tilted and she smiled sadly. "Howard told me things didn't end well between you. I'm not one to say I told ya so."

Thanks. And well, you just did.

"And despite... what happened...." She meant with me taking her to the future. "You're always welcome here. Now come on in. I'm starving."

THE NEXT DAY I went to work for Faye again, sweeping hair, dusting shelves and restocking them. I listened to her patrons gossip about their neighbors and the latest Hollywood scandal. My ears were perked, listening for the sounds of Howard's truck. Or worse, Dan peeking his nose in.

I jumped every time the phone rang, before I remembered that I'd given Dan Faye's house number, not the salon number.

A whole twenty-four hours passed without a peep from Dan. My stomach churned with worry. I could go back at any time, and I had no idea where this wayward juvenile was. I took a walk after dinner, looking for him, but didn't see any sign. I considered going back to the school, but couldn't imagine why he'd go there. I came across a nearby hostel and though they recognized Dan when I described him, they didn't know where he was.

At least I could assume he was still alive.

At supper time the next day, I heard the familiar sound of Howard's truck driving in the yard. I broke out into a sweat. I felt my eyes popping out of my head as I stared at Faye.

"I can't see him. I'm sorry." I zipped to the bathroom to hide.

Howard's voice boomed through the house. "Hey, Faye. Any leftovers?"

I cracked the door open just a sliver. My heart still did those crazy somersaults at the sight of him, all bronzed and buffed from working outside.

"Uh, sure," Faye said. "Have a seat."

Howard pulled a chair out but then stopped. His gaze settled on my half-finished plate.

"You got company?"

Faye's eyes darted toward me and I quietly closed the door.

"*She's* here?" I heard him say. "I'll just take it to go then, if you don't mind."

I swallowed and forced back tears. Gotta *love* rejection.

DESPITE HOWARD'S propensity for dropping in at Faye's unannounced, I did think that everything would work out okay, more or less, (assuming I got Dan back in one piece and could administer some kind of miraculous memory erasing technique). When I was here I'd just work for Faye, try to keep out of trouble and make sure to stay away from boys.

I *thought* it would all be fine until Faye hit me with this.

"I'm getting married." She told me this on our lunch break the next day, just before taking a bite of her egg salad sandwich on white bread, while staring out the window.

"To Larry?" I couldn't keep the astonishment out of my voice.

"Yes, who else?"

"Why? Do you love him?"

"Enough. Love can grow over time, and I love him enough. He's good and kind and adventurous. We both know we won't have children together, and I'd be happy to be a step-mother to his two kids at least."

Faye took the milk bottle and topped off her glass. "Larry wants to travel to Europe on our honeymoon."

She stared at me, wanting me to understand the bigger picture. "I want to see the world, Adeline, before it changes."

Before it changes into the mess it was in my time. I swallowed. "When?"

"Soon. A small ceremony at the courthouse. We don't want a big affair. We've both had that before. We just want to quietly get married and start our lives together. Betty is going to be my witness. Larry's brother will be the second one we need."

"When?" I said again.

"Tomorrow."

Tomorrow? That definitely came under the heading of "soon." And she was just telling me this now?

"Don't worry, you can stay here anytime you want, whether I'm here or not."

She lowered the remainder of her sandwich to her plate and came to me. It'd been a long time since she'd shown me any physical affection and I welcomed her arms as they wrapped around me.

"As odd as things are," Faye said, stroking my hair. "I find I have a lot of affection in my heart for you, like a daughter."

"Thanks, Faye." I fought back a mixed bag of emotion. It was the kindest, nicest thing she could say. "It means a lot to me. And not just because I need a place to sleep."

"I know, dear. I know. So be happy for me, okay?"

Here was the funny thing; I was happy for her. I found myself smiling. "Larry is a lucky man."

"And I am a lucky woman. Tomorrow, I'll be Mrs. Larry Bradshaw."

What? *Bradshaw?*

My brain ticker ran on high speed. Couldn't be. Could it? Was Faye Mrs. Bradshaw, the old lady who lived next door?

I examined Faye's face, trying to picture what she would look like as a senior citizen.

"Why y'staring at me like that?" she said.

SINCE FAYE WAS SHUTTING down her shop while she was on her honeymoon, I was now out of a job. I supposed I could go back to selling jewelry like I had in Cambridge. At least I didn't have to worry about a place to stay, and Faye had recently bought groceries so I had food for a while. Lots of frozen TV dinners.

I said goodbye to Faye mid morning when Larry picked her up to get married. I think he was surprised at how nice I was to him since I hadn't exactly made him feel welcome before. But I understood now that this was for the best. Faye belonged in this world, not in mine.

Now that I had nothing pressing to do, I found myself lounging on the sofa in my pajamas, hugging a pillow. I was startled by the sound of the door opening, and I wondered if Faye had forgotten something, or maybe had changed her mind.

It wasn't Faye. It was Dan Highland.

"Where have you been?" I said with a very parental tone when I saw him. "I've searched high and low for you."

He sauntered across the living room like he had every right to be there and settled into one of the chairs. I didn't like how his eyes narrowed as he stared at me. Even though I had PJs on. I held a sofa cushion tight against my chest. We were alone in the house and I wondered if I was actually safe here with

Dan. My heart scuttled around like a bag of beads falling to the ground.

"Faye's in the salon," I lied.

"No she's not. I saw her leave with some guy. Pretty fancy duds for a Saturday morning."

On closer inspection, Dan didn't look so good. His hair was greasy and not the Brylcreem hair-gel kind. Dark circles shadowed his eyes.

"You don't look that hot," I said.

"Yeah, well, I haven't exactly slept much, since I, like, *time traveled*."

"It gets easier with practice."

"How long have you been doing this?"

Like I was going to tell him anything about my life. "Long enough."

"So, can you take me back now? I'm kind of done here."

"I can't control when it happens. But I get a little warning from this end. I just have to grab your hand in time."

"Then I better hang around for a while."

I didn't like the sound of that at all. "You can't. Faye's going to be back soon."

"She had suitcases."

"What? Were you spying on me?"

"Uh, ya. As much as we both hate the notion, I need you right now."

Sad but true.

"Look, do you got grub?" Dan rubbed his belly. "I'm starving."

I felt a little nudge of pity. He did look pretty pathetic. "Toast and eggs okay?"

"Sounds heavenly."

I left Dan in the living room and got to work on cooking us brunch. I hadn't eaten either and suddenly felt starved. I was spreading butter on the toast when I heard the side door open and I thought Dan was going out for some reason.

"Hey, it's almost..."

I turned around and stiffened. Howard stood there in all his studly glory. His eyes washed over my bed-head appearance and I wished I'd at least washed my face.

"Hi," I said.

Howard didn't say anything as he reached for an apple on the counter, his eyes not leaving mine.

I was more than a little unnerved. I stirred the eggs while they scrambled. Howard chomped on his apple until he reached the core then tossed it into the trash.

"You didn't get invited either," he finally said.

To the wedding he meant. So much seemed to go on around me all the time, I couldn't keep the threads in my life straight. I shook my head. "No."

"I don't know what her big hurry is." I shrugged. I might've had something to do with that, but I couldn't get into it with him.

"She's off to see the world, so I figured it would be a good time for me to go, too."

A little wave of panic rolled through me. Even though I knew nothing could ever become of me and Howard as a couple, he was the only one I really knew here, outside of Faye. Even Judy was gone now, with her plans to study acting.

"Where would you go?"

"Nashville. The music scene is crazy there. I have a better chance of makin' it there, than here, I think. I only hung around this long because of Faye. Now she has Larry, I'm not needed here."

He stood up abruptly and walked straight to the door. "Gotta run, kid," he said. He'd never called me that before. I guess he could read the expression on my face, that part of me still wanted him. He put me in my place.

"Faye says she's letting you hang out here when your ol'man's gone. I don't see what difference it makes which empty house you stay in, but hey, maybe I'll see you around."

"Howard?" I went to the door, and stood in the space between the living room and the kitchen. He stopped for me, but I didn't know what to say.

His expression was soft, but then it suddenly hardened. His eyes narrowed as his gaze settled on something over my shoulder.

Not something, some*one*.

Howard's presence still made my mind go numb and I'd totally forgotten about Dan Highland waiting in the living room.

"Whats'up?" Dan said.

Howard's eyes darted back at me. "Who's that?"

"Oh, he's no one. Just a... not even a friend."

"Hey, thanks Adeline," Dan said. "Is that grub almost ready."

"You're feeding him? Faye's food?"

"I uh..."

Howard closed the door and stepped back inside. "You're not dressed for male company, Adeline," he said. "I think I'll show your guest out."

Dan was on his feet in a flash and before I could stop him, Howard had Dan by the cuff of his shirt. Dan wasn't one to go down without a fight. They crumbled to the floor and knocked Faye's pictures off the wall.

Guys. It seemed like I was always breaking up some kind of fight these days.

I bent down to pull on Howard's arm. He inadvertently knocked me in the shoulder with his elbow. I rubbed the bruise, my head spinning from the sharp pain. I smelled something burning and rushed to pull the blackened eggs off the stove before I accidentally burned Faye's house down on top of everything else.

I felt the blast of light and groaned.

I was standing alone in the short hallway of Hollywood High dressed in my faux, fifties skirt and present-day shoes.

I'd left Dan Highland in 1955 in Faye's living room, fighting with Howard.

TWENTY-ONE

OH, FREAK, oh freak, oh freak.

What else could I do to screw things up? People were going to notice that Dan Highland was missing. He was popular. Or at least notorious.

I couldn't remember what class I was supposed to be in and I knew I was late regardless. I snuck out of the school and caught a bus home.

By the next day, Dan Highland was big news. Everyone buzzed about his disappearance at school. Even the cops came around to ask questions, though none of his thuggy friends thought to implicate me. By six o'clock, he'd made the local news.

There was nothing I could do about Dan's disappearance for now. I was assuming that Howard didn't actually kill him, and that Dan had brains enough to keep out of trouble while keeping watch for me. I soon as I got back, I'd find Dan and not let him out of my sight until I brought him home, safe if not sound.

Neither Marco nor Bluebell had been taking the bus, and I felt like a leper. I'd alienated my only two friends and I supposed I was getting what I deserved—the company of Bing and Bong who sat in front of me and shot spit balls across the aisle and out an open window like twelve-year-olds.

My life was too messed up for real, meaningful relationships anyway.

I spent the day keeping to myself and trying to focus on my school work. The last thing I needed on top of everything else was bad grades and my dad breathing down my back because of them.

I kept my eyes peeled for Marco and finally had a sighting after school. It seemed like years since we hung out, and I was surprised at how much I missed him. He was on the steps with the skaters, effortlessly manipulating his skateboard with his feet. I leaned against the fence to watch. I didn't know why I never noticed how good looking he was before. It was just so blatantly over-the-top obvious to me now. His strength and determination, his faithfulness to his family and friends, all qualities that sparkled with movie star brightness, now that it was too late.

Facts were we never had a chance anyway. With me and my traveling issues, and his impending move, I had to accept it wasn't meant to be, but I couldn't shake the sorrow and disappointment that settled over me

Marco glanced my way and caught me watching him. He offered a sad smile, and my heart almost broke. Then he turned back to his skate friends and I boarded the bus by myself when it came. Bluebell was missing again, too. I didn't think she was talking to me anymore anyway. Her greeting was less than enthusiastic at lunch and she left as soon as I sat down.

I had my arms wrapped around my books and pressed them tightly against my chest. I dragged my feet, not exactly excited to go home to an empty house. Dad had gotten a small part in a commercial, which apparently was going to take sixteen hours to shoot.

He was really excited about his first paying gig. I tried to be happy for him, but all I could see was a future with him working and me at home alone eating frozen, store bought meals cooked in the microwave.

"Adeline?"

It was my name, but I didn't recognize the voice. I stopped and looked around. All I could see were the street kids setting up to play ball hockey and an old guy in a cap sitting on one of the benches in the green space.

I kept walking.

"Adeline Savoy!"

I turned sharply in the direction of the voice. It was coming from the old man on the bench.

I took tentative steps toward him, my eyes bugging as recognition registered.

"Dan Highland?"

I didn't think there was anything left that could happen to me that would surprise me, but I was wrong.

The old man laughed. "Yes it's me. Come sit down. We have a lot to talk about."

I honestly couldn't believe my eyes.

"Dan, you're..."

"Old. I know."

My legs felt shaky and I took Dan up on his offer to sit.

"I wanted to catch you before you try to come back for

me," he said. I still couldn't get used to his low, gravelly senior's voice.

"But you're missing; people are looking for you."

Dan guffawed. "So, my foster parents won't care. Trust me, they'll be relieved."

"But, you made the news."

Dan waved an old, gnarly hand as if that was an insignificant detail.

"If you bring me back, I'll miss out on the life I just lived, won't I?" he said. "All of that will just disappear."

I had a terrible thought. I hadn't really taken a good look at the news since I'd gotten back. I hadn't had a chance to check if the world had changed because of Dan Highland.

"What did you do? Are you filthy rich now? Did you fraud the system with privileged knowledge of the future?"

He chuckled. "No, Adeline. I didn't change anything. I kept to myself. I had a quiet happy life."

I leaned back and stared at the senior version of Dan skeptically. "That doesn't sound like the Dan Highland I know."

"It's not."

"What happened to you then? What caused this .... change of character?"

The wrinkles around his dark eyes fanned wider and I swear they twinkled.

"Don't tell me. You fell in love?"

"I did." His smile faded and a flash of sadness shadowed his face. "She's gone now, but I wouldn't trade those years for the world. Not even for the chance to be young again."

"Are you sure?"

"Positive. In fact, I want to thank you, Adeline. Truly, I have no regrets. Oh, and I'm very sorry for being a jerk to you when I was young. It's a lifetime ago to me when I was such a punk, but I realize it was just a few days ago for you."

"What have you been doing all these years?"

"I fell in love, got married, had a child."

"Really?" Should I be worried? I still didn't know for sure if Dan or his child hadn't changed history in some way. "I mean, that's great and all, but, Dan, it wasn't supposed to be you."

"Who says? Maybe it was destiny that you took me back and I lived my life in an earlier less complicated time. The world didn't stop. No wars fought on my account."

I sat back and stared at him—his receding hairline, the leathery wrinkled skin that sagged on his face. My mind still couldn't comprehend that this Dan and the Dan I'd left fighting with Howard two days ago was the same person.

"Well, I'm glad things worked out for you," I finally said. "And if I happen to run into a younger version of you some-time, I'll just wave."

Dan released a throaty chuckle. "Sounds good." He groaned and grabbed at his back as he got to his feet. He tipped his hat and left me to ponder how strange my life was.

WHEN DAD CAME HOME LATER that night, I turned off the TV and called him over to join me in the living room. Meeting up with old Dan Highland made me realize some-thing. I didn't want any regrets at the end of my life, and right now I had plenty.

"How was your day?" I asked.

"Long. You do a lot more standing around and waiting

than you would think. But, it was a good experience and at least now I have something solid to add to my résumé."

"Hmm. That's good."

"Hey. Is everything okay?" he said, sliding into a seat opposite me on our puffy, leather sectional.

I fiddled with my fingers. My nerves were jumping. I wanted to talk to my dad and I didn't even know for sure what I was going to say.

"Adeline? What's up?"

I looked him in the eyes. They were hazel, almost brown. Not at all like mine. They squinted with concern.

"I'm mad at you, Dad."

"Why?" He seemed sincerely taken aback by this.

"Because, when you said moving to Hollywood would give us more time to be together, I believed you. But nothing's really changed between us since we moved here. We live in the same house but have different lives. I want a father, not a roommate."

He ran a hand through his hair and breathed out heavily through his nose.

"You're right. I've been completely unfair to you." He paused, then said, "To be honest, it's hard for me to be around you."

"What?" That hurt. "Why?"

He swallowed. "Because you look so much like your mother. The older you get, the more like her you become."

His eyes grew red and glassy and he pinched them closed. For the first time, I actually felt bad for him.

"I try to be friends with other women, hoping that maybe I'll forget her, at least a little. I want to move on."

He looked at me then. "It's not working."

"Oh, Dad."

"I need you to forgive me. In my efforts to get over the loss of your mother, I'm afraid I've lost you, too."

A tear escaped from his eye. I'd never seen a man cry before, and it killed me to see my dad in so much pain.

"I forgive you," I peeped. My throat tightened and my eyes got all scratchy. "Can you forgive me? I'd only thought about how Mom's death had affected me. I didn't even consider that you could still be hurting over her."

"Come here, Sweetie."

We met each other half way and squeezed each other tight. In that moment, the angry monster in my gut took a blow.

THE NEXT DAY Mrs. Bradshaw waved me over again. I hadn't seen her outside since I'd figured out that she was Faye. I was a little nervous to see her. I wondered if she remembered me.

Melissa was there with her, so at least we wouldn't spend the whole time in awkward silence. She poured us all tea, and we made pleasant conversation about the weather and the neighborhood.

"Has Mrs. Bradshaw lived here long?" I asked.

"She was one of the first ones to move in," Melissa said after sipping her tea. "In fact, she called the developer up personally asking for this specific lot, even though there were cheaper ones available in an earlier phase."

I smiled at Faye. She'd picked this house because she knew I would eventually move in next door.

"What happened to Mr. Bradshaw?"

"My uncle Larry passed away ten years ago from cancer. He and Auntie Faye were married for almost fifty years."

I winked at Faye. "Nicely done, Mrs. Bradshaw."

Now for the question I was dying to ask, but scared to. I sipped my tea.

Faye must have read my mind. "Ho-ward?" she said.

"Howard? Aunt Faye?" Melissa asked. "What about him?"

I confess, I'd googled him. There were more Howard Walkers in the world than you'd think, and the one I was searching for was probably too old for the web. I didn't find anything newsworthy about any of the Howard Walkers out there, and nothing to pinpoint that I had found the right one.

"Howard is Aunt Faye's brother," Melissa explained. "He's not related to me by blood." This fact seemed important for her to point out.

"Uh, what happened to him?"

"Oh, he's fine, I guess. Lives in Nashville. Wanted to break into the music biz once upon a time, or so the story goes. He ended up becoming a sound man. Got married a couple times, went to rehab for alcohol and gambling. A couple times. Never really amounted to much."

I couldn't help but look at Faye and get her reaction to this less than rosy assessment of Howard's life. She was looking under the table, like there was something there that fascinated her. She wouldn't catch my eyes.

A dark Mercedes drove up and parked in the driveway of my house. I excused myself, telling Faye/Mrs. Bradshaw, I'd come again soon. The back door of the car opened and Bluebell wiggled out.

"Hey," I said, not keeping the surprise out of my voice.

"I'm running errands with my chauffeur. You got a minute?"

"Yeah, sure."

I opened the front door and let Bluebell hobble in before me. I showed her to the kitchen and offered her a glass of ginger ale, which she accepted.

"Is your driver..."

"He'll wait."

She slugged back her drink and set the empty cup on the table.

"I'm cutting you some slack, Adeline, because I realize that you don't understand what it's like to live with a handicap. Your epic insensitivity is due to your epic ignorance."

Ouch. I took her admonishment on the chin, but she was wrong about that. I did understand what it was like to live with a handicap. If time travel wasn't a handicap, then I didn't know what was.

"But, what you did the other day, standing up to Dan Highland? That was cool."

I smiled. "It was overdue. I know I have a history of being a sucky friend, but I want to change that."

"I'm glad. And I mean I'm sorry the guy's missing, and I hope he's okay, but he was a supreme jerk."

My mind jumped to my meeting with old Dan the day before. "My gut tells me everything will work out as it should."

Bluebell stood and dragged her leg over to me. I tensed when she hugged me until I was certain my sweater was doing its job of covering my skin.

"Wow, Ad, you are wound-up." Bluebell sat down and pulled a book out of her backpack. "I bought this for you because I know you like the fifties."

She handed me a hard cover book full of glossy pictures taken from the fifties. "This is great, Bluebell." My eyes welled up a little from this random act of kindness.

"Yeah, well, look at this picture." She flipped it open and pointed at a girl in a blue, flared skirt sitting on a narrow, leather sofa. "She looks just like you!"

I grinned. That's because it *was* me. This was taken at Benny's party. Judy sat beside me, laughing, her mouth stretched wide over straight white teeth. I'd bet she hated this picture. It was probably taken by that guy who'd trailed William Shatner.

Bluebell's eyes were wide with expectation. "Well?"

"It does kind of look like me."

"I know, weird right?"

If she only knew.

TWENTY-TWO

I WAS HOME ALONE the next day when someone tapped sharply on the front door. I opened it to find Marco standing there, fists in pockets, sun-kissed curls hanging low on his forehead, his lips spread wide across his face.

"We're not moving!"

I gasped. "Really?"

"Yeah, really. Poser finally revealed his true colors, so Mom turned the job down."

This strange sensation bubbled up in my tummy. I thought it was called joy. "Oh Marco, I'm so happy for you!" Before I could stop myself I wrapped my arms around him and spun him in a circle.

"Hey." He pulled back and ducked a bit to look at me. "Who is this and what did you do with my neighbor? Just kidding. Happiness looks good on you."

I laughed. "I think I'm going to try it out more often."

I was finally getting it. This was my life, here and now, in the twenty-first century. I belonged *here*, in this Spanish villa with lemon trees and cacti in the front yard, with my dad and the boy next door.

We needed to celebrate, and I knew the perfect thing.

"Let's go to the beach."

Marco gave me one of those corner-of-the-eye stares. "Are you sure? You don't really have a good track record there."

"Yes, I'm sure." I grabbed a hoodie and put it on. "Let's go before we miss the next bus."

I felt like skipping and I had to hold myself back from looking like a child. Though it was the exact same bus route we'd taken before, everything looked different to me. Lighter, brighter. Marco noticed my change in mood and brushed his shoulder against mine.

"What's gotten into you?"

"Nothing." I played coy. It wasn't like I could tell him about my epiphany.

"You're just glad you're not going to lose me as a neighbor."

"Nah..." I joked. "Though, I would miss your chocolate cookies."

For a change, the beach was empty. The surf rental shacks were shut down and all the food kiosks were gone for the winter. We walked along the shore, short of getting our feet wet until we found a dry spot and sat down.

I watched Marco gaze out over the ocean, the wind blowing his hair across his face. He brushed it out of his eyes.

"Bluebell told me you stuck up for her at school a couple days ago. Actually, took on Dan Highland."

"Well..." I scooped a fistful of sand and let it sift through my fingers.

"That was cool."

"Um, thanks."

"I wonder what happened to him? So weird for him to go missing like that."

I just shrugged. Dan Highland's secret was safe with me.

Marco's eyes met mine. "Coming here was a great idea. Thanks for dragging me out."

"No problem." I felt something in me jump, a little wave in my gut, something...happy. Because Marco wasn't moving away, and maybe we'd still have a chance.

"Hey, I have something for you," I said. "A present. I was going to give it to you as a going away gift, but now it's a 'Yay, you're not moving' gift."

I loved how Marco's eyes sparkled with expectation. "What is it then?"

I pulled out the paper I'd slipped into my back pocket and handed it to him.

He shot me a perplexed look before opening it. His mouth dropped.

"Where'd you get this?"

He was staring at the entertainment flyer from Curos 1955. There was a picture of Carl Rodney on it and underneath, his autograph.

"I have my sources," I said mysteriously.

"Wow. This is really... wow. Thank you."

Our eyes locked. Major electricity zipped up and down my spine and I thought my heart might stop.

Marco's expression didn't change. His palm rested on the sand between us. Then, he slowly wiggled his fingers and crab walked his hand across the distance between us, stopping halfway. I knew what he wanted, or at least what he thought he wanted. I crab walked my hand to meet his, stopping shy of touching his fingers.

My heart kicked into gear and jumped madly in my chest. Could I do this? Risk a trip back to the fifties with Marco as my guest?

It hadn't killed Faye when she traveled with me here, and I'd gotten her back home in one piece. And Dan seemed to do all right, too.

I imagined arriving in Faye's world with Marco. Would he freak out? Would he still like me the way he claimed?

There was only one way to find out.

"Are you sure you're up for the adventure?" I said.

His lips formed that smirky grin I'd grown to love. "I'm so sure."

He didn't know what he was saying, but I hoped he was right. I held my breath as I closed the gap between our hands, and weaved my fingers through his.

Skin on skin.

If you enjoyed reading *Like Clockwork*, please help others enjoy it too.

Lend it: This ebook is lending-enabled, so please share with a friend.

Recommend it: Help others find the book by recommending it to friends, readers' groups, discussion boards and by suggesting it to your local library.

Review it: Please tell other readers why you

liked   this   book   by   reviewing   it   at
leestraussbooks.com

Don't miss COUNTER CLOCKWISE!

Casey and Nate are back!

HIGH SCHOOL *senior Casey Donovan is in trouble. Again. If only she had trusted in Nate's loyalty when he traveled to Spain with his college basketball team - despite being accompanied by the cheerleading squad and Fiona the Floozy who'd made it super clear she wanted Nate for herself. Then she wouldn't have made that impulsive trip to Hollywood and let Austin do that stupid thing that threatened her relationship with Nate, and triggered a trip into the past.*

Only something is wildly wrong. She's not in the 1860s like she should be. It's 1929. And she didn't come alone.

Shop at leestraussbooks.com

Read on for an excerpt.

FOR MORE INFORMATION about my books or how to follow me on social media, visit leestraussbooks.com

ABOUT THE AUTHOR

Lee Strauss is a USA TODAY bestselling author of The Ginger Gold Mysteries series, The Higgins & Hawke Mystery series, The Rosa Reed Mystery series (cozy historical mysteries), A Nursery Rhyme Mystery series (mystery suspense), The Light & Love series (sweet romance), The Clockwise Collection (YA time travel romance), and young adult historical fiction with over a million books read. She has titles published in German and French, and a growing audio library.

When Lee's not writing or reading she likes to cycle, hike, and stare at the ocean. She loves to drink caffè lattes and red wines in exotic places, and eat dark chocolate anywhere.

For more info on books by Lee Strauss and her social media links, visit leestraussbooks.com. To make sure you don't miss the next new release, be sure to sign up for her readers' list!

Discuss the books, ask questions, share your opinions. Fun giveaways! Join the Lee Strauss Readers' Group on Facebook for more info.

Did you know you can follow your favourite authors on Bookbub? If you subscribe to Bookbub — (and if you don't, why don't you? - They'll send you daily emails alerting you to sales and new releases on just the kind of books you like to read!) — follow me to make sure you don't miss the next Ginger Gold Mystery!

www.leestraussbooks.com
leestraussbooks@gmail.com

COUNTER CLOCKWISE

CHAPTER ONE

SO WHAT IF he was going to Europe with his college basketball team without me? So what if the cheerleading squad and head cheerleader, Fiona Frias the Floozy, was going too? So what???

I stared hard at the text message from Nate Mackenzie, my hot boyfriend of one year, nine months and five days. My college-all-star-athlete-first-string-forward-for-the-Boston-University-Terriers-basketball-team boyfriend.

Nate: It's official! We're going to Spain!! It was a close call with some passport issues, but just got word we're all clear to go!

All those exclamation marks were like stakes in my heart. Spikes to my feet. I felt frozen on the spot in the middle of a busy hallway in Cambridge High. Bodies brushed by wafting stale air and teen sweat, but it wasn't enough to propel me. My heart weighed heavy like an anchor and a scratchy lump formed in my throat.

Nate had promised me all my firsts, but the one first he could never give me was international travel. I couldn't fly. There was always the possibility that I could trip—swirl back in time—and it was best if my feet were firmly planted on the ground when that happened.

So he was going to Europe without me. Big deal. If I wanted Nate in my life (and I did!), I had to make some concessions. I couldn't tie him down, guilt him into not doing things just because I couldn't.

I forced myself to text him back.

Casey: That's great. The Terriers are great. You'll do great.

Nate: I'm glad you think it's GREAT.

Casey: Are the cheerleaders going too?

I winced as I pressed send, immediately wishing I could

take it back. This was the crux of my issue with Nate going to Spain and we both knew it. Fiona Frias, college girl, long-legged, green-eyed, Latin beauty was in love with my boyfriend and she didn't try to keep it a secret. At all.

Despite Nate's reassurances, I felt completely insecure. Here I was, still in high school, while Nate was halfway through his degree. Of course other girls would notice him. Of course other girls would chase him. Girls who were more mature and experienced than I was. Unscrupulous girls.

Girl. It wasn't fair to group all girls together. Just one girl. Just one unscrupulous girl.

It only took one.

Nate didn't text back right away and I knew I upset him with the question. For him it was an issue of trust, and all my overt and obvious inquiries about Fiona made him believe I didn't trust him.

I did trust him. It was *her* I didn't trust.

My phone finally pinged with his response.

Nate: Yes.

Only one word. Only one word! Gah! That was all he had to say? Nothing to comfort me and calm my worries?

Casey: That's Great!

The bell rang and snapped me back to reality. Lucinda, my best friend who seriously deserved a medal for willingly wearing that moniker, poked my arm. "You're going to be late." Then, seeing my face, she asked, "What's wrong?"

"Nate's going to Spain. With *her*."

We started walking down the hall toward my creative writing class. Lucinda's history class was across the hall. She knew all about my worries over Fiona Frias and the impending team trip to Spain. She shot me a look of concern—or maybe it was pity—before saying, "I think you're boiling things down a little too low."

"Am I? Nate will need the self-control of a saint to resist her over there," I said. "For one thing, the drinking age is lower and well, a guy's power of resistance goes down with each drink, and it's a million miles and several time zones away. Fiona..."

"Casey!" Lucinda grabbed my arm and forced me to look down into her dark, worried gaze. "Nate loves you. He's not going to do anything with Fiona. You have to trust him."

"I know. You're right." I felt like an idiot. When did I turn into this crazy, jealous maniac?

I made it to my seat in Mr. Ryerson's creative writing class just as the bell rang. I folded my long limbs under the desk, brushed dark runaway curls off my face and took a deep breath. Lucinda was right. I was overreacting. I hid my phone under the desk and texted quickly before Mr. R confiscated my phone.

Casey: I really am happy for you. Promise to send me lots of pics.

Nate: Of course. I don't leave until next week. I'll see you tomorrow night.

Tomorrow was Friday, and Nate had promised to come to Cambridge until he had to leave for practice on Saturday afternoon. It wasn't a lot of time but it was better than nothing.

Casey: love you

Nate: ly2

I let out a breath of relief. We were okay.

Nate would be gone for two weeks. It wasn't like we saw a

lot of each other now anyway. We both had school and homework and jobs. With texting and Facebook, it would be like he
wasn't even gone.

Mr. Ryerson petted his thick graying mustache as he called
the class to order. I loved this class. Writing was something I
could do as a time traveler without too much worry. For the
most part it was a job of solitude. I didn't have to worry about
touching someone, skin-to-skin, and accidentally taking them
back in time. Only four people knew about my "gift." Lucinda,
who was the first unlucky person to go back with me and also
how I learned about the skin to skin thing; Nate, who wasn't
my boyfriend at the time and my brother Timothy, both of
whom were also accidental traveling guests; and Samuel, a
fellow traveler. The only other one I knew.

No, that wasn't true. There was that blond girl I met in the
convenience store one time. Adeline? I wondered what
happened to her and if she had a good-looking boyfriend who
was being chased by another older, prettier girl.

I wasn't sure what kind of living I could make as a writer,
but this class offered unit studies in several fields: journalism,
poetry, short stories, novels, memoirs (mine would sound like
fiction!) and scriptwriting.

"The deadline for your deposit on the Hollywood trip is
today," Mr. Ryerson said, eyeing me specifically. I'd signed up
back in November with no intention of actually following
through. I only wanted to avoid the inevitable questions as to
why I didn't want to go. I *did* want to go, but the class was
flying. What if I tripped while in midair? It would be
disastrous.

I broke eye contact with Mr. Ryerson and stared resolutely
at my desk. Mr. Ryerson continued, "We're joining a script-

writing class with students from Hollywood High and we'll visit all the tourist traps. Bring your laptops. Leave your winter coats."

A cheer went up in the room. I slunk lower into my seat, once again awash with discouragement.

"Casey?" Mr. Ryerson called my name and I snapped to attention. He stood at my shoulder and I looked up, past his bushy mustache and into his squinty, concerned eyes. He leaned in and lowered his voice. "Are you having trouble coming up with the deposit?"

It was like I suddenly had bionic hearing and caught the sounds of the other twenty-eight students quieting and cocking their heads toward me. "Yeah," I whispered back. "I don't think I can go."

"It's possible the school could come up with a subsidy."

It was so quiet in the classroom, Mr. Ryerson's words echoed off the wall. My cheeks flushed with embarrassment. Now everyone thought my family had money problems. I squeaked out, "No, that's fine."

"You're a good writer, Casey." He dropped a paper on my desk with a big red A+ on the top. "I'd hate to see you miss out."

I spent the class period working on a short film script about a stupid contemporary boy who gets stuck in the civil war era and joins the Union Army (write what you know!). I couldn't resist checking my phone when the lunch bell rang. I got a new Instagram pic from FabulousFiona! It was a selfie. Her abundant bosom peeked out of her cheerleader uniform (some things just aren't handed out fairly!) A couple basketball players chatted in the background. I recognized one of the guys as Nate.

Her comment: "Too bad you can't come."

I gasped. Fiona Frias just made this personal! My thumbs went into high speed and I immediately forwarded the image to Nate.

Casey: This!!!

He didn't text back. Of course, he was busy playing basketball while Fiona jumped up and down on the sidelines in a short skirt and there was nothing, NOTHING, I could do about it.

The thought of her traveling to Spain with Nate (I know, it was with the basketball team, but SHE thought it was with Nate) made my blood boil. I had to be careful or I was going to stress myself back to 1863 and I really didn't feel like dealing with that right now. I stopped at the fountain and sipped cool water, long and hard.

Breathe, Casey.

Once my heartbeat was under control I leaned against the wall and wiped my face with my sleeve.

Maybe I couldn't go to Spain with Nate and maybe I couldn't stop Fiona from going with him, but I could control some things in my life. I walked resolutely back to my creative writing class. I had a checking account and an unused crumpled check in my purse. I'd written only a couple checks in my life, but I remembered how. I gripped my pen tightly as I wrote the date, the amount required for the deposit and then scribbled my signature at the bottom with a flourish. I swallowed hard. I was going to Hollywood.

Shop leestraussbooks.com

MORE FROM LEE STRAUSS

Shop at leestraussbooks.com

GINGER GOLD MYSTERY SERIES (cozy 1920s historical)

Cozy. Charming. Filled with Bright Young Things. This Jazz Age murder mystery will entertain and delight you with its 1920s flair and pizzazz!

Murder on the SS Rosa

Murder at Hartigan House

Murder at Bray Manor

Murder at Feathers & Flair

Murder at the Mortuary

Murder at Kensington Gardens

Murder at St. George's Church

The Wedding of Ginger & Basil

Murder Aboard the Flying Scotsman

Murder at the Boat Club

Murder on Eaton Square

Murder by Plum Pudding

Murder on Fleet Street

Murder at Brighton Beach

Murder in Hyde Park

Murder at the Royal Albert Hall

Murder in Belgravia

Murder on Mallowan Court

Murder at the Savoy

Murder at the Circus

Murder in France

Murder at Yuletide

Murder at Madame Tussauds

LADY GOLD INVESTIGATES (Ginger Gold companion short stories)

Volume 1

Volume 2

Volume 3

Volume 4

Volume 5

HIGGINS & HAWKE MYSTERY SERIES (cozy 1930s historical)

The 1930s meets Rizzoli & Isles in this friendship depression era cozy mystery series.

Death at the Tavern

Death on the Tower

Death on Hanover

Death by Dancing

THE ROSA REED MYSTERIES

(1950s cozy historical)

Murder at High Tide

Murder on the Boardwalk

Murder at the Bomb Shelter

Murder on Location

Murder and Rock 'n Roll

Murder at the Races

Murder at the Dude Ranch

Murder in London

Murder at the Fiesta

Murder at the Weddings

A NURSERY RHYME MYSTERY
SERIES(mystery/sci fi)

Marlow finds himself teamed up with intelligent and savvy Sage Farrell, a girl so far out of his league he feels blinded in her presence - literally - damned glasses! Together they work to find the identity of @gingerbreadman. Can they stop the killer before he strikes again?

Gingerbread Man

Life Is but a Dream

Hickory Dickory Dock

Twinkle Little Star

LIGHT & LOVE (sweet romance)

Set in the dazzling charm of Europe, follow Katja, Gabriella, Eva, Anna and Belle as they find strength, hope and love.

Love Song

Your Love is Sweet

In Light of Us

Lying in Starlight

PLAYING WITH MATCHES (WW2 history/romance)

A sobering but hopeful journey about how one young German boy copes with the war and propaganda. Based on true events.

A Piece of Blue String (companion short story)

THE CLOCKWISE COLLECTION (YA time travel romance)

Casey Donovan has issues: hair, height and uncontrollable trips to the 19th century! And now this ~ she's accidentally taken Nate Mackenzie, the cutest boy in the school, back in time. Awkward.

Clockwise

Clockwiser

Like Clockwork

Counter Clockwise

Clockwork Crazy

Clocked (companion novella)

Standalones

Seaweed

Love, Tink

ACKNOWLEDGEMENTS

To the fans of the Clockwise series, thanks so much for loving Casey first and taking a chance on Adeline. That fact that you are reading this series (and the acknowledgments!) makes me want to jump up and cheer!

To my family and friends, I couldn't do any of it without you, (especially my beta reader and proof reader friends–you know who you are!)

And, as always, my deepest thanks to God for blessing me with a life where I can sit around in my PJs and make up stories in my head.